TIME THIEF

CHRISTOPHER MALINGER

POLAR PHOTOGRAPHY PUBLISHING

Time Thief
By
Christopher Malinger

www.christophermalinger.com
Cover design by Polar Photography
www.polarphotography.com
In cooperation with Sean Malinger
Image (Tunnel Vision) provided by Jean Hutter
www.jeanmhutter.com
Graphics provided by Shutterstock_1191616963

ISBN: 13-978-1-7362446-1-6
ISBN: 10-7362446-1-2

"Son, the greatest trick the Devil pulled was convincing the world, there was only one of him."
David Wong

CHAPTER ONE

"Bad Stuff Always Happens at Night"

"Shh," Kyle whispered.

"I told you, dumb-ass," Adam fired back, "the watchman is takin' a booze snooze."

Kyle's tall, lean frame hugged the wall like a rat creeping along a gutter. "I don't like it. It's too ruzky."

Adam, in the lead, walked with his shoulder only inches away from the brick wall. He stopped and turned to Kyle. "Peep this, dude. I've cased the joint. It's butter. Now come on, and I don't want to hear any more of your whining."

The alleyway dead-ended. The only entry was through a remote-controlled chain-link gate over a security fence on the far end. The metal fencing, augmented with three rows of barbed wire, was an easy task to cut. Cautiously, Adam stood on top of the fence, reached up, and draped a scarf over the security camera.

"There, now we're safe."

"Hey man, ain't the watchman gonna notice that?"

"Ha, the guy's a real lewser."

Headlights of sporadically passing cars flashed past the gated end, prompting the interlopers to pause momentarily. Besides the infrequent street movement, the rustling of dead leaves over the alley's pavement heightened their uneasiness.

The duo moved slowly in tandem within the alleyway's shadow. Ahead lay a row of storage units. Each roll-up door, bathed faintly in a pale umbrella from the security lights, appeared secured from any unwanted foray. Only one remained masked in the gossamer shelter of night.

Adam looked at Kyle with an air of triumph. "Hey, no moon. Great for a heist. Like I told you, easy as light cheese."

Kyle grunted, then followed Adam.

Adam paused in front of the unlit unit and pushed back his soiled Milwaukee Brewer's cap to the rear of his head. He pulled out a bolt cutter strapped inside his navy blue pea coat, then drew close to the side lock.

"Here, hold this lock while I take a bite with my master key," he said with a chuckle.

Moving alongside Adam, Kyle nervously adjusted his blue-knit watch cap. He pulled out a pair of dirty cotton gloves from his heavily scuffed brown leather jacket. After slipping them on, he grabbed the lock to hold it steady.

"Ascared of getting your hands dirty?" taunted Adam.

"No, Man. It's friggin cold."

Adam opened the jaws of the bolt cutter then pressed them deeply against the shackle. Grunting, he squeezed the two arms of the tool, his arms shaking under the pressure. The lock gave way with one swift crack. Laying aside the cutter, he impatiently watched as Kyle removed the severed lock from the hasp.

They hurriedly lifted the door. The torsion spring protested with a whine along with the squeal of the rollers as they raised it only high enough for them to slip under the bottom steel plate. With equal swiftness, the door closed, and the blackness of the interior encased them.

A metallic clang echoed inside as Kyle threw away the broken lock.

Adam fumbled in his coat pocket for his flashlight.

"I can't see a thing," complained Kyle.

"Relax the cacks, Jack." Adam flipped on the beam into Kyle's face.

Kyle covered his face with a hand. "Hey, man, whadda you do that for?"

"Soory." Adam dropped the beam onto the floor. With a jerking movement, he started to explore the interior. "What ... " Adam froze, his shaft fixed on a single chair in the center of the storage space.

"I thought you said there was valuable shit in here."

Adam shook his head. "I was casing the place for weeks. I saw these guys bring in tons of stuff that looked really valuable."

"All I see is this weirdo chair," said Kyle as he drew closer to the center of the room.

Adam kept his flashlight's beam focused on the strange-looking chair, crafted of black walnut wood. The back and seat, upholstered with a light-blue, subtly patterned damask linen, appeared worn. It possessed an air of power. The armrests seemed designed for functionality rather than relaxation.

Kyle reached out and gently stroked the armrest. He drew back as if stunned.

"What's the matter?" asked Adam.

"I dunno. It feels ... electrical."

"Can't be. It ain't plugged in."

"Feel it yourself if you don't believe me."

Adam shot Kyle a scowl of distrust then cautiously touched it.

"It tingles!" He drew back his hand.

"I told you."

With theatrical bravado, Adam once more touched the chair but did not recoil. His hand caressed the back, then followed its contour to the front. "Wow, it feels ... it feels like it's alive."

"Maybe it's some sort of a magic chair?"

"Ha, and you belong in a circus."

"What are we gonna do now?" asked Kyle.

"Don't know. I suppose we can take the chair. If nothing else, we can hock it."

"We can always use another chair in our man-cave," Kyle said and sat down.

Adam watched in puzzlement as Kyle kicked and squirmed. His contortions appeared pain-driven, yet his face looked as if he was in ecstasy. Kyle leaped out of the chair. "What a ride," he exclaimed.

"What did you feel?"

"Hell, I was flying for hours."

"Hours?"

"Yeah, hours. What did you do while I was gone?"

"Gone? Where to?"

"I don't know. I was just flying ... yeah, I was just flying. Try it. You'll see," Kyle prodded.

"You're bucknutty. You expect me to believe that crap? You're just trying to punk me."

Kyle motioned toward the chair. "Hey, I ain't blowing fairy dust up your skirt. If you don't believe me, you try it. You'll see."

Adam carefully examined the chair with his flashlight. He tested the seat, then sat back. The light fell from his hand, hitting the concrete with such force that it went out.

Kyle heard the seemingly uncontrolled shaking of Adam. In a panic, he dove onto the floor and madly felt for the flashlight. Kyle located it and pushed on the switch. Aiming the beam of light on him, he watched Adam's body flail about in an apparent seizure. Out of caution, he moved back until Adam appeared to regain control, then jump off the chair.

"Geeze, what a ride!"

"I told you."

"Man, do you know what we have here?" Adam cried. "We're gonna have us more gold than Michael Phelps."

"Michael, who?"

"Never mind, dumb-ass. We gotta get this chair outta here."

As Adam and Kyle gripped the chair, they were both filled with panic as a surge of power shot through them like lightning.

"Whoa!" Adam exclaimed as he let loose of the chair.

"What the hell was that?" yelled Kyle, equally stunned, recoiling backward.

"Maybe it doesn't want to be moved?" Adam took out a pair of leather gloves from his pocket and slipped them on. He cautiously touched an armrest. "Hey, nothing. Looks like we gotta handle this thing with OJ's. Come on, Kyle put your wimp skins on, and let's bail."

Kyle slipped on his gloves and lifted one end of the chair while Adam took the other side. Once outside, they again blended into the shadows and hurriedly made their way back to the chain-link fence.

Kyle was the first one to put down his end. "Hey, man, how do you expect us to get this chair over to the other side?"

"How the hell did I know we'd be hauling Lazyboy shit?" Adam fired back and began to take off his pea coat. Setting his tools aside, he placed his coat over the fence. "It ain't heavy. Grab a side. Help me prop one end of the chair on the top rail." With the chair tilting partially over the support, Adam jumped to the other side. "Okay, push it over to me."

Kyle handed Adam the tools with the chair safely in place, removed the scarf covering the camera, and then joined him. Adam jerked his coat free and quickly put it on. "Damn, I'm cold," he said as he buttoned up. When Adam reached for the bottom button, it was missing. "Shit," he grumbled under his breath.

"What's wrong now?"

"Nothin'," Adam muttered.

Their beat-up green, Ford Ranger, was parked on a backstreet. After sliding the ornate chair onto the short bed truck, Adam and Kyle lifted the tailgate. To obscure their catch, they pulled out a paint-stained drop cloth from the back of the extended cab. Using the Ranger's step-side for ease of access, they reached down and tucked the fabric under the chair, spreading the remaining sheet over the rest of the cargo. Making use of a length of clothesline, they anchored it in place before speeding off.

———

An odd noise stirred the watchman to waken. He wasn't conscious of the peculiarity of the sound, only of its subconscious power to arouse. Rising from a recycled army cot, he stretched. Following a trip to the bathroom, he peered outside through slightly sloping blinds and peered down the long, shadowy alleyway. Glancing over his shoulder at the wall clock, he figured it was probably a good time to make one of his infrequent rounds. Reluctantly, he pulled on his blue, down-hooded jacket, grabbed a flashlight, and before stepping outside, drew the hood over his head.

The watchman, his breath visible in the cold, damp air, followed his usual routine down the center of the alley, randomly whipping the beam of his flashlight over the storage lockers. When he came to the end of the row, he spotted the last unit's empty hasp.

"Shit," he said to himself and quickly moved to the roll-up door. He placed the lit flashlight on the ground. Hoisting the door, the light from the flashlight slid along the cement floor to reveal an empty locker.

The watchman rushed back to his office and pulled the registration directory from the top center drawer of his desk. He already knew the renter, but not the phone number. Now his hands trembled with fright as he put the handset to his ear. He punched in the number. The phone tolled several times before being answered.

"Yeah, who is this?" the raspy voice on the other end demanded.

"Mr. Angelo, it's Chuck, the watchman."

"Why you calling me at this time of night?"

"It's your storage unit ... someone broke into it."

Chuck held the earpiece away from him while he heard a deluged of profanities.

CHAPTER TWO

"Be Careful What You Ask For"

Adam and Kyle carefully maneuvered the chair up the twisted staircase. When the duo reached their apartment, they paused long enough for Adam to unlock the door. Once inside, they set it in the foyer.

Without a word, Adam went to the refrigerator, slipped off his gloves, and took out two cans of Carling Black Label beer. He flipped one to Kyle, who unintentionally let it slip through his gloved hands.

"Hey man, at least tell me when you're going to toss me one." Kyle shoved his cotton gloves into his pocket. He picked up the can and popped it open. A spray of foam gushed out. "See, look what you did," Kyle yelled before putting his mouth on the lid.

"Quit your bitchin. We're victorating our new swag. Drink up." With his beer in hand, Adam moved past the mismatched kitchen dining set, sink full of dirty dishes, and into the small parlor.

The room held an eclectic collection of junk. An outdated pin-up calendar hung in the narrow wall-space between the two front windows. Below it sat a chipped silver-painted radiator, tarnished by age and neglect. A brown, overstuffed corduroy chair occupied one of the corners. Strips of gray duct tape, on its armrests, served as bandages to mend the years of abuse. Opposite the chair, an old-style TV console served as the foundation for a flat-screen television. Where the cathode ray tube and electronic innards once resided, the void now contained a library of skin magazines.

Adam surveyed his domain and sipped his beer. He eyed the faux leather couch littered with old newspapers.

Still slobbering on his can, Kyle moved next to him. He gulped his drink loudly, then belched. "You thinkin' 'bout dumping that?"

Adam turned abruptly to Kyle. "Listen, genius, where do you suppose we're gonna nap? No, I'm thinking we'll have to move it and make room." He put down his beer on the coffee table adorned with sticky rings, residues from previous beverages, filled ashtrays, and more porn magazines. "Here, grab an end and help me."

Kyle pushed, and Adam pulled until there was sufficient room for the new addition. "Let's get the chair," ordered Adam.

Other than the coffee table, their furniture took on the appearance of a defensive barrier hugging the walls like Conestoga wagons around a prairie encampment. The new chair, with its clean upholstery, stuck out into the room like an incompatible appendage.

Retrieving his can of beer, Kyle asked, "Now what?"

Adam, his face contorted in serious deliberation, stroked his stubble. He finally said, "We gotta test this thing again. Maybe it won't work now that we've moved it?"

"You want me to go for another ride?"

"Yeah, why don't you hop on her and take her for another spin."

"Hey man, it's better than shrooming. I gotta take a whizz first."

While Kyle was tending to his call of nature, Adam fondled an armrest. A tinge of power traveled up his arm and across his back. He stepped away. There was something different in the way the chair reacted to his touch than earlier in the storage locker. He carefully stepped within reach of the chair and gently touched it again with his index finger. Like a static electrical shock, only more severe, it snapped back, leaving Adam with a painful blister.

The rush of the flushing toilet proceeded Kyle's return. "Okay, man, the tank's drained. Let me at her."

Adam, still stunned and uncertain if he should say anything, only nodded.

"Ya know, we could get rich selling rides on that thing," Kyle said as he approached.

"Uh-hu," Adam mumbled uneasily.

Kyle, still wearing his watch cap, eagerly jumped back into the chair. With hands gripping the armrests in palpable fear, he moved as if he were on a rollercoaster. Kyle's head jerked from side to side, and his eyes widened in panic. He screamed. His cap flew off his head, and then he was motionless.

Adam, frozen with fright, gawked at Kyle's limp body. "Hey, man! You all right?" Gradually, Adam inched his way toward the chair. He reached out, touching Kyle's leg hesitantly, only to be thrown back, as if hit by lightning. Adam's arms flailed about wildly, unable to grab hold of anything to lessen his momentum before smashing into the wall.

CHAPTER THREE

"I Know A Guy"

The sky revealed the gloominess of an approaching storm as Tony "The Cat" Angelo, arrived in his black Mercedes. Stephen, his driver, wearing a black leather jacket, dark-blue dress slacks, and heavily cushioned brown shoes, held the rear door open as his boss exited the vehicle. Stephen was big and imposing. Doubling as a bodyguard, any would-be assailant would think twice about taking him on. Stephen gave the deserted alleyway the once-over.

Tony, displaying an impatient scowl, was dressed in a black Hart Schaffner Marx overcoat, matching fedora, and highly polished Florsheim shoes. The only item in contrast to his ensemble was the white silk scarf around his neck. It hung open in front, draping loosely over his broad shoulders. Tony's wardrobe, in essence, mimicked his idol James Cagney from the movie *Public Enemy*. He viewed the film several years after its first introduction when he saw it as a teenager and was fascinated by Cagney's style and mobster persona.

Unlike this tough-guy image, his moniker was conferred on him by a rival gang. It wasn't meant as a compliment, but his effeminate way of delicately walking. Like "Bugsy Siegel," he hated his nickname, and no one ever dared say it to his face.

Tony paused outside the watchman's shack and inhaled the early morning pong of Jones Island. To most, it was an unpleasant smell. But to Tony, it harkened back to an earlier time in his life. He smiled in his remembrance when it was a hodge-podge of fishing shacks, coal yards, heaps of scrap metal, and oil storage tanks interspersed among the gravel roads and train tracks. Here is where it all began—breaking into railroad cars and outsmarting the railroad dicks.

Chuck, the watchman, was already standing at attention as Tony walked in. "Good morning, Mr. Angelo," he said, with uncertainty, a tone balanced between a statement and a question.

"Is it?"

"Mr. Angelo, I can ex—"

"Cut the crap. Grab your flashlight. We're going for a walk."

Chuck, still in his down-filled jacket, retrieved the flashlight from his pocket. "I have it here," he said, waving it in the air.

"Let's go."

Gingerly moving past Tony Angelo, Chuck led the way outside. He spotted Angelo's driver leaning against the Mercedes, enjoying a cigarette. Chuck avoided eye contact and turned down the alley.

"You want me to follow you, boss?" the driver asked.

"Na. Stick close to the gate."

Tony Angelo's trailing footsteps put the watchman on edge. He expected that at any moment, he would be knocked out or shot in the back. He was tense, and the absence of conversation only heightened his unease. Reaching the last storage unit, Chuck whipped the flashlight out of his pocket and trained it on the empty hasp.

Tony looked up at the burned-out bulb. "Why is that out?"

Chuck cleared his throat. "Ahem ... it must have just happened."

Tony Angelo pointed at the unshackled hasp. "Open it up."

The rollers squealed as Chuck raised the door.

Angelo gave Chuck a penetrating gaze. "You didn't hear that?"

"I ... I must have been in the can."

"Gimme that light," Angelo demanded and jerked it out of Chuck's hand.

The dim morning light was slowly inching its way into the storage locker, yet it wasn't sufficient to penetrate the deep interior. Tony Angelo's light licked the back wall, then move slowly along all three sides. The beam froze over the remnants of a lock.

"Get that," Tony ordered.

Chuck snatched up the severed padlock and handed them to Angelo.

Holding the pieces in his gloved hand, he said, "I want them bastards who done this." He balled his hand into a tight fist and threw the lock against the metal back wall. The noise reverberated within the locker.

"I want them dead. You got that, Chuck?"

Chuck nodded submissively. "Yes, Mr. Angelo."

"Let's go back to your shack and check the security videos."

Chuck shifted uneasily in place.

Tony Angelo turned toward the watchman, who froze in hesitation. "You do leave the cameras on, don't you?"

Ashen-faced, Chuck nodded hesitantly. "I think so."

"What do you mean, 'I think so?'"

"The other day, Richie, the daytime guard, tells me that he thinks the camera facing Bay Street was a little glitchy."

"Glitchy?"

"Yeah ... it's, ah, it's a little funny at times."

Tony abruptly turned and drew closer to Chuck. "By funny, you mean it doesn't always work?"

"Yes, Mr. Angelo. Richie and I thought it would fix itself, so we didn't want to bother you."

Angelo pointed an accusatory finger at Chuck. "Listen, I pay you guys to look after this place. When something like that happens, you call. *Capisce?*"

"Yes, Mr. Angelo," Chuck answered timidly.

"Good. Now how the hell did these bums get in here in the first place?"

"I swear on my mother's grave that they didn't get through the front gate."

Angelo motioned. "Come on, let's check the back."

Chuck moved outside and stared at the overcast sky as a light mist fell on his face. Without mentioning the weather, he dropped his gaze and guided Tony Angelo to the small back lot behind the storage lockers. When they turned the corner, Chuck noticed strands of barbed wire hanging limply over the chain-linked fence.

"Well, it doesn't take a rocket scientist to guess how these bastards got in. When was the last time you checked back here?"

"I dunno. Maybe a week ago."

Tony Angelo held one of the severed wires. "Snipped clean with wire-cutters," he said as he twisted the wire in his gloved hand briefly before letting it go. Tony pulled off his right glove and reached down to pick up something in a patch of weeds clustered near the fence. "This doesn't look like it's been out here too long." He held it out in the palm of his hand. "You have any idea where this came from?"

Chuck took it and examined it. "It's a button from a peacoat. Lots of longshoremen and sailors wear 'em," he said while handing it back. "That anchor stamped in the button is a dead give-a-way."

Tony Angelo slipped it into his pocket. "Okay, let's see what's on the video tape."

Stephen was standing outside, leaning against the watchman's shack, while smoking a cigarette under the front canopy's protective covering. He straightened up as Tony started up the stairs. He flipped the butt into the driveway, then held the door for his boss but released it as Chuck began to enter. Chuck checked the shutting with his hand and shot Stephen a glance of resentment.

Tony removed his coat and hat. Before draping them over a chair, he shook off the few beads of rainwater. "You got any fresh coffee?" he asked gruffly.

"I made it about an hour ago, but I can make up a fresh batch."

"Never mind. Gimme some of that stuff for now."

Chuck retrieved a clean mug, and with an unsteady hand, took the pot off the hotplate and filled the cup. "Black?" he asked shyly.

"Yeah, that's fine." Tony took the mug and blew lightly over the steamy brew. "Okay, let's see that tape."

Walking to the back of the shed, Chuck opened the small closet next to the bathroom. The recorder was old, but Tony believed in frugality, living by the maxim, "If it ain't broken, don't try to fix it." While he reversed the recorder, Tony Angelo sat at the desk and watched the frames rapidly retreat over the television screen. The whirling noise ceased when Chuck hit the stop button and pushed play.

"Mr. Angelo, I started the tape the same time I took over from Richie."

Tony stared at the screen as the alternating view from four security cameras danced back and forth. Occasionally a rat or feral cat would scoot over the frame, supplemented with darting shadows of passing traffic.

"Stop," shouted Tony as he leaned closer to the monitor. "Back it up."

Chuck reversed the feed then slowly advance it.

"Stop right there," Tony ordered. "Now, go back a little. Okay, okay, now freeze it." There was a blurry image of the top of someone's head wearing a Milwaukee Brewers cap on the screen.

CHAPTER FOUR

"No Regrets"

Adam, dazed and in pain, lifted himself off the rug. He rubbed his head and tried to get his bearings. He wasn't suffering from amnesia because everything looked familiar, except his apartment continued to move as if he were on a ship. All the furniture was intact, including the new chair. What puzzled him was the absence of Kyle.

"Hey, man," Adam called out. "Why did you leave me on the floor?"

Except for the drone of early morning traffic from the street below, the silence in his empty living room hung heavily in the air. As Adam staggered around, he noticed Kyle's knit watch cap lying on the side of the new chair. He stooped over to retrieve it. When he drew it closer, he detected a strange smell. It was like a whiff of a lightning strike in a spring shower.

Adam pitched the cap aside, moved back, and stared at the chair. Remembering his last encounter, he considered his options and the blister from touching the chair. He picked up a broom that leaned against the tarnished radiator. Grasping the broom handle, Adam aimed the wood pole at the chair. Slowly he moved closer until it was within striking distance, then gently tapped the chair's arm. Nothing happened.

Frustrated, he forcefully flung the broom at the chair. Hitting it with a loud snap, it evaporated into thin air. Alarmed, Adam recoiled in fear. Not believing his eyes, he began to move wildly through his apartment.

He called out, "Kyle, you're pulling some shit on me. Come out, you bastard. It ain't funny."

Terrified and confused, he checked every possible hiding place in their flat before collapsing onto the couch. He began staring at the ceiling, thinking about his next move. With an afterthought, he got up, keeping his distance from the chair, and went to the refrigerator. He pulled out two bottles of beer, stopped, returned to the fridge, and grabbed one more before going back to the couch.

Adam twisted off the first bottlecap and tossed it at the chair. The bottlecap sizzled and popped before disappearing.

"What the hell?" he said, then guzzled down his first bottle.

———

Stunned, Kyle jumped free from the chair and staggered to his feet. Uncertain of his surroundings, he cautiously moved toward the only light source—three small windows set within a large gable. The floor groaned under his weight as he sniffed the musty air. Daylight began to fade as he pressed his face to the center glass, which was cloudy with age. Kyle used the sleeve of his jacket to wipe away the grime. Again, he peered out and saw nothing but the thick cover of forest blocking any view beyond its tall pines and contorted oak tree branches. He tried the other two windows without success as the landscape melted into the encroaching nightfall.

Something scampered behind him. He turned. Remembering the flashlight he had in his coat pocket, he pulled it out and aimed it into the darkness. The beam struck a raccoon, which momentarily froze in its glow before dashing away. Kyle continued to explore the interior of what appeared to be an attic. He reached the middle of its cavernous loft, where he found a trapdoor. He directed his flashlight down the open stairwell. Within the accumulation of dirt on the stair treads existed clear evidence of previous travelers. The footsteps looked fresh, and Kyle started to follow the dusty trail. He considered yelling out but held his tongue, fearful of who might answer.

Kyle unbolted a door and found himself on a balcony bordered by a balustrade. He crept to the edge of the opening and looked down onto the hall below. Fragments of debris littered its floor, with traces of recent activity crisscrossing the rubble underneath. He hesitated and decided to go back upstairs, uncertain how long his light would hold out or who he might encounter.

Retracing his steps, he wished Adam was around to give him support. He swept the entire attic with his light, but the darkness swallowed its feeble beam. Kyle searched for a suitable spot to sleep until dawn. Only the chair remained. As he debated his resting place, he caught sight of a couple of bottle caps and a broom, all of which, Kyle was certain, were not there when he left.

———

Adam raised a hand to deflect the sunlight. He glanced at the clock through squinting eyelids and saw it was a couple of notches before nine. He rolled onto his side, faced the back of the couch, and drew himself into a fetal position. Adam was about to close his eyes when he heard a shuffling sound. He moved slightly, turned his head, and saw Kyle standing, his feet set wide, holding a broom. Adam spun around and shifted into a sitting position.

"Where the hell you been?"

"Don't know."

Adam rose. "Whadda mean, you don't know?"

"I'm thirsty."

"D'ya wanna beer?"

"Yeah," said Kyle, who began to move toward the kitchen.

With a cold bottle of beer in his hand, Kyle sat down on the closest kitchen chair.

Adam sat opposite, eagerly waiting for something that made sense.

"I'll tell you, man—it was like … it was like trippin'." Kyle took a long swig. "After sitting in that chair," he pointed toward the living room, "I went straight to the *Addams' Family* house."

"You're farting through your mouth."

Kyle shook his head, then took another swallow. "Listen, like I said, this place looked like the Addams' mansion, 'cept it ain't got no Lurch."

"Okay, so say I believe you. What did you see?"

Scrunching his face in apparent deep thought, Kyle leaned back. "There's this chair … like the one we found. I jumped out of it. I start to check it out this creepy place. It's empty, nothing but a shit-hole … junk all over."

"Hey man, you said it was empty. Listen up dillhole, what kinda junk?"

Kyle shook his head. "Nah. I mean dirt, shit like that. It hadn't been vacuumed in a few donkey's years."

"Did you case the place completely? Like, did you see any furniture —you know, crap like that?"

"I did an Alcatraz sweep with my flashlight, and I saw a lot of closed doors. Maybe there was stuff behind them. I don't know. I was thinkin' my light was going to go to sleep, so I went back upstairs into the attic."

"Then what?" Adam asked, rivetted to the tale.

"Then, nothin'. I looked for a place to crash. I was scared to get back in the chair, so I sat down and leaned against one of the walls. When I woke up, I was hungry and thirsty. I figured, what the hell, and took my chances in the chair."

"And?"

"And, here I is." Kyle made a ta-dah motion with his opened arms.

Adam put his elbows on the table and cradled his face in his hands.

"Whatcha thinkin', Adam?"

Adam pulled back and cupped the rear of his head with both hands. "Why did you bring the broom?"

"I didn't bring it back with me. I tested the chair with it. When it popped-a-Houdini, I figured I'd give it a try, too."

"Humm." Adam stroked his stubble. "I think you may have discovered a way to make us rich."

CHAPTER FIVE

"We're Gonna Be Rich"

"Listen, man," Adam said, trying to get Kyle's attention.

Kyle looked up from his dinner, which consisted of a messy sub-sandwich of ham and cheese garnished with lettuce and tomatoes. A bit of the mayonnaise oozed out and clung to his right cheek. "Whadda want?" he asked with a packed mouth.

"When you get done filling your pie hole, we're going on a trip."

Kyle wiped his mouth with the back of his hand and took a sip of Coke. "Ya mean, on that flying chair?"

"You got it, Einstein."

"Whadda want from me?"

"You're gonna be my Robin in this caper. We'll case this Addams' place and see what treasure we can haul back. I figure we can score something and fence the stuff. Think about it. I'm guessing this place ain't around here, so we got that on our side. We get in, and we get out. It's a perfect crime."

"What if we get busted wherever this place is?" asked Kyle before taking another bite.

"You said the place looked deserted."

"Yeah, like Scary Movie 2."

"Hell, there ain't no ghosts or shit like that in real life. It's all play pretend—Hollywood crap." Adam got up. "When you're done slobbering down your food, come into the other room."

The chair looked harmless, but Adam knew it had powers beyond anything he had ever encountered. He picked up a section of the newspaper and flipped it onto the armchair. *Poof!* It vanished.

Cautiously walking past, Adam went into his bedroom. He pulled open a dresser drawer and rummaged around before finding his LED flashlight. After more digging, he located a couple of batteries. Adam unscrewed the back of the light and inserted the cells. He flicked the switch and aimed the beam at the ceiling before shutting it off. Satisfied, Adam began to go back into the living room but paused.

Without much reflection, he returned to the dresser, dropped to his knees, and removed the bottom drawer. Setting it aside, Adam lay flat on the linoleum floor and reached to the back of the cavity to retrieve a snub-nosed .38 caliber revolver. Assuming a sitting position, he opened its cylinder, eyeballed the five rounds, and snapped it closed. He grabbed a fistful of bullets before putting the drawer back in place. Adam shoved the weapon into his waistband and returned to the living room.

Entering the room, Adam watched as Kyle's eyes focused on the grip of his gun protruding from his waistband.

"You gonna pack a toolie on this job?"

"I ain't taking no chances. Did you change the batteries in your flashlight?" asked Adam.

"Yeah, man. I even snapped up extras." He patted his right cargo pants pocket. "And a couple of Snickers bars, too." Kyle tapped his left leg.

Adam gestured toward the chair. "Well, Einstein, seeing you know the way."

"No problemo," Kyle said and approached the chair. "I gotta tell you something first."

"What, you gotta pee?"

"Nah, nothin' like dat. When I came back, the trip was a piece of cake—nothin' like the first time. Maybe it got used to me?"

"Yeah, maybe it did, like me getting used to you."

They both laughed.

"Okay, what's keeping you? Get on with it," Adam ordered.

With his back to the chair, Kyle, wearing an army fatigue jacket and blue-knit watch cap, gave a parting wave and dropped backward. Like the newspaper, he vanished.

A bit hesitant, Adam moved into position. His hands became moist, and he felt his pulse quicken. Crossing his hands over his chest, like a swimmer doing a backward plunge, Adam, in his peacoat and Brewers cap, followed.

To his surprise, Adam wasn't forcefully ejected into another dimension but found himself lying peacefully on a duplicate chair, staring at bare rafters. He shifted his attention to Kyle, who was standing in front of him. Unsure of the consequences if he stayed put, he scrambled to his feet.

"Okay, now what?" Kyle asked.

Adam was about to say something but instead moved toward the window at the end of the gable. Gazing outside at the night sky with its full moon illuminating the grounds below, he asked, "Wasn't it around noon when we left?"

"Yep," Kyle said as he moved next to Adam. "It was the same way when I took the trip."

"I don't suppose you have any idea where this place is, do you?"

"Like I sez, it was getting' dark and didn't have much light to go snoopin'."

Adam removed some of the window's grime with the palm of his hand. "You're right—this place is kinda creepy," he said, eyeing the dense forest below, before turning away. "C'mon, let's see what we can find in this dump."

"The door to the downstairs is over here," Kyle said and turned on his flashlight aiming its beam toward the center of the attic. Adam trailed behind, watching the light bob from side to side as they walked through a cordon of old chests.

While descending the narrow staircase, Adam felt along the walls. "I don't suppose you found any light switches when you were here?"

"I didn't want to blow my cover, so I never looked for any."

When they reached the balcony, bordered by a railing, Adam exclaimed, "Holy shit, this place has got to be over a hundred years old." The light from his flashlight flayed wildly at the closed doors on the second floor. "You never tried any of these doors?"

"Nah, kinda scared of what was on the udder side."

With their rays of light leading the way, Adam and Kyle located another staircase leading to the main floor. Each step generated a mournful cry from the dry treads until they reached the bottom. Like the stairs, the floorboards groaned under their weight. On their left was an open hearth littered with the remains of past fires. Shuffling their way to the center of the immense lobby,

Adam pointed his shaft of light on one singular looking door. "Let's try that one."

All the doorways and trim were richly carved within the hall's interior. Adam selected the one that received considerably more artistic effort and attention to detail.

"What all them funny words?" asked Kyle.

"It's Latin."

"What does it say?"

"It says, 'Whoever enters will die.'"

Kyle froze. "I ain't going in there."

"Shuddup, dumb-ass, I was only joking. If I knew what it said, I'd be working in some university, not trying to score in some creepy mansion. C'mon."

Adam leaned his shoulder against the door and began to turn the ornate knob. Before the door moved, they heard the unmistakable sound of approaching hooves. Startled by the unexpected night visitor, they abandoned their attempt and sought shelter in a nearby alcove.

CHAPTER SIX

"The Hunt"

Giovanni sat restfully in his barber's chair, his face buried in the morning newspaper. He lowered the paper at the sound of the bell over the transom. Setting the paper aside, he jumped to attention. "Mr. Angelo, good morning." He waved a welcoming hand toward the chair. "Please, have a seat."

Tony Angelo removed his overcoat, then suit coat, and gave it to his bodyguard Stephen, who hung them on the nearby coat rack. As Tony mounted the chair, Giovanni took a fresh seersucker barber's cloth from the cabinet and shook it open. He uneasily watched as Stephen went back to the entrance and flipped the shop sign to close. After drawing the shade over the door's window, he closed the blinds on the main window. Before finding a spot to rest, Stephen grabbed the paper Giovanni had recently discarded.

Giovanni draped the barber cloth over Tony and asked, "I'm surprised to see you so soon, Mr. Angelo." He wrapped a tissue strip around Tony's neck then tightened the cloth.

"Yeah, I know. I had a rough morning and didn't have time—only a shave today."

Someone, ignoring the closed sign, tried the door.

Giovanni inserted the headrest and tipped back the chair. He placed a towel over the front of Tony and turned on the hot water faucet of the sink. "So, Mr. Angelo, you look a little upset. Anything wrong?"

Tony cleared his throat. "Yeah, someone broke into one of my storage lockers near Jones Island."

"Did they steal a lot of stuff?"

"Let's just say they got something important. Besides me needing a shave, that's the real reason I came here."

Giovanni tested the water then began to soak a barber towel in the sink. He glanced at Tony's bodyguard. "Ahh, Mr. Angelo, you don't think I had anything to do with it, do you?"

"Relax. I'm not accusing you. I'm only saying what happened."

After wringing the towel, Giovanni placed it over Tony's face and breathed a sigh of relief. He moved back to the sink and began to lather up the shaving cup.

An uneasy silence permeated the barbershop. After removing the hot towel, Giovanni began applying the shaving cream. "You said, 'that's why I came here.' What do you mean?"

"You know a lot of what goes on in the neighborhood. I'm thinking you might know who did the break-in."

With one hand holding the shaving brush, the other open in defense, Giovanni backed away slightly. "Hey, Mr. Angelo, I don't need any trouble. I run a good business and keep my nose clean."

"You're not paying attention. I only meant you probably cut the guy's hair."

Giovanni lowered his hands, placed the brush back into the shaving cup, and retrieved the razor. "Do you have any idea who this guy is?"

"That's why I'm here. I was hoping you could tell me. I'm figuring these bums know the territory. You know, locals."

Giovanni fought to control the slight tremor in his hand as he began to shave Tony. The traffic outside, normally unnoticeable, now became a roar under the silence.

Tony remained quiet as Giovanni worked the razor under his nose.

"Do you have any idea who broke into your place, other than it could be someone from the neighborhood?" Giovanni asked, drawing back his razor.

"I have two clues. One, the guy wears a Brewers cap and the other one, he's probably missing a button on his navy peacoat."

Giovanni laughed. "There's only one person who wears anything like that around here—Adam Cabano."

Tony's eyes lit up, and he turned toward Giovanni. "Any idea where this guy lives?"

"Mr. Angelo, you relax and let me finish shaving you while I tell you what I know."

"Okay, educate me."

"See, this Adam Cabano thinks of himself as an operator. When he struts in here, he acts like Sinatra, all full of himself—you know, doing it his way. Well, he sold me some gear a while back. Nothing much, only some barber supply things. I figured the stuff was hot. I've been cutting his hair for years. Anyway, he comes in here maybe once every four weeks or so. He used to live in the Bay View area, beginning when he was a punk kid. I guess he got used to me. He's got a buddy that never shuts up. I don't recall his last name—Kyle, something or other." Giovanni wiped his razor on the towel lying on Tony's chest.

"You got any idea where these bums live?"

Giovanni shrugged. "I'm not sure. When the two of them come in here, they talk a lot about pool hustling. I think they hang out somewhere around First and Mitchell. He did live off KK some years ago. Now he lives on Lapham. I forgot the cross-street."

Stephen set the newspaper off to the side.

"When was the last time you saw them?" asked Tony.

"Around three weeks ago." Giovanni tipped back Tony's chin and resumed shaving.

Giovanni glanced at Stephen, who appeared interested in the conversation. There was an uneasy silence broken only by the slow, grating of the razor against Tony's neck. Giovanni's hand became moist under the pressure of Stephen's scrutiny. Finished, he wiped Tony's face with the towel and began to run water in the sink.

"I don't suppose you know what kind of car these guys drive?"

His back turned to Tony, Giovanni immersed the towel in the sink while tempering the water. "He's got an old beater Ford truck. I don't know the year, but it's green."

Another customer tried the door.

"Stephen, give Giovanni my card."

"Sure thing, Boss."

Giovanni squeezed out the towel and placed it on Tony's face.

Reaching out to take the card, Giovanni, his hands still moist, took it with his thumb and index finger along its edges. He eyed it and glanced back at Stephen.

Without a word, Stephen turned away, returned to his seat, and retrieved his paper.

Giovanni slid the card into his shirt's pocket and moved back to the sink.

Tony removed the towel from his face and handed it to Giovanni. "Here, take this and give me a splash of your best aftershave."

Without hesitation, Giovanni took the towel, threw it in the sink before reaching high onto the shelf for his premium cologne. He splashed a few drops onto his hand and massaged Tony's face.

Tony stepped down from the barber's chair and moved close to the mirror over the sink to admire himself. Still looking into the mirror, he said, "Next time those bums come into your shop, give me a call. *Capisce?*"

"Yes, Mr. Angelo."

Stephen helped Tony with his suitcoat. After adjusting the coat, Tony reached into his breast pocket and took out his wallet. He peeled off a hundred-dollar bill, handed it to Giovanni, and smiled. "Nice shave."

"Thank you, Mr. Angelo."

"Now, don't breathe a word about this to anyone. I don't want to spook those bastards. When they come in here, if we don't get to them first, I want you to stall them. When I get here, I'm going to teach them a lesson they'll never forget."

CHAPTER SEVEN

"Welcome to the Dude Ranch"

Still hidden in the alcove at the front of the house, Kyle leaned over Adam's shoulder. Straining to get a look, both men tried to discern who the nightrider was. Only the silhouette of the stranger, back-lighted by the moon, was distinct. Undoubtedly male in his deport-ment, his boots struck the wood floor with confidence as he made his way in the direction of the mysterious door that only moments ago they attempted to breach. No doubt alerted by the sound of the man's arrival, the sculpted door yawned opened, bathing both the greeter and visitor in warm, amber light. As the bearded man approached the doorway, he removed a squat-looking, hourglass-shaped top hat and transferred it to his other hand that also held a riding crop. The caller was the first to extend a hand.

"Joseph, your arrival on this late of an hour is indeed unexpected. I wasn't anticipating you until tomorrow," the short, rotund man said as he reached out in greeting.

"My good man, my eagerness to see what treasures you have for me outweigh my need for sleep. Byron, lead the way," Joseph said, gesturing toward the lit interior.

The door closed with a thud, driving the foyer back into its moonlit state.

"There's something that ain't right about this shit," Kyle said as he eased back away from Adam.

"No shit, Sherlock."

"Why are those guys dressed so funny?"

Adam shook his head. "That's a good question. I don't know. Maybe they're going to a masquerade party. C'mon, let's take a walk outside."

"For what?"

"That door is too thick for us to hear anything."

Kyle, close behind Adam, tiptoed out the front door. Outside, they spotted the visitor's mount tied to a cast-iron, hitching post. The horse snorted as they passed. Stealthily, they made their way around the enormous house. Guided by the moon's glow, they reached the only windowpane that displayed any light.

"The window's too high," Adam said as he scanned the area for something to stand on. In the distance, he spotted a wood and cast iron garden bench. He pointed. "That should work."

Breathing heavily, they set the bench against the foundation wall.

Adam, winded, hopped onto the top of the bench. "Yeah, whoever built it, built it to last," he said quietly before stretching to reach the windowsill. Cupping his hands around the ledge, Adam was only inches away from seeing the interior. While keeping a firm grip on the window ledge, he positioned one of his feet on the bench's backrest and pushed himself up. With the interior in full view, he gasped at what he saw. For several moments Adam stood gawking at the scene, precariously balancing himself without uttering a word.

"Whaddaya, see?" Kyle asked eagerly.

Adam turned his head and looked down. "Shuddup," he hissed and resumed peering inside.

"C'mon, lemme have a look," Kyle begged, pulling his way onto the bench.

"Okay, okay, but shut your yap."

Trading places, Kyle murmured, "Holy shit," while standing tiptoed precariously, trying to get a better footing. His leather-soled boots, damp from the evening's dew, slipped off the bench. He collided with Adam.

"What the hell," Adam groaned while shoving Kyle away.

"Hey, man, I'm sorry."

Adam jumped to his feet. "My gun, you stupid idiot, where's my gun?"

Kyle, still on the ground, rolled onto his knees and began combing through the tall grass.

"Shit!" barked Adam. "Dammit, sounds like someone's coming toward the window. We gotta split."

Remaining close to the foundation and in the shadows, they bolted like roaches caught in the sudden light. Adam glanced back at the window—framed in its amber glow, a dim shadow moved.

Reaching the edge of the building, they ran headlong toward a series of outbuildings that angled away from the manor. Although bathed in the moon's glow, Adam felt confident they remained unseen.

Adam, in the lead, selected the larger of the three buildings. Panting heavily, he opened a four-panel door set near an end of the brick structure, while Kyle brought up the rear.

"This place smells like horseshit," Kyle uttered in disgust as he closed the door behind him.

In the cavernous blackness, a low, guttural pulsating noise greeted them.

"What the hell was that?" Kyle asked.

Adam laughed. "If the smell of this place is any clue, I'd say it was a horse."

Kyle turned on his flashlight. "Are we on some sort of a dude ranch?"

A horse snorted.

"Shut that damn thing off," Adam commanded.

"Aren't you going back for your toolie?"

"Those guys may be outside looking to see who made that noise when we took our tumble. Besides, I'm tired. C'mon, let's find us a spot to crash until dawn."

Kyle's boots echoed on the stone floor while Adam's sneakers made a flopping noise. Several of the horses derisively snorted as the nighttime intruders passed between the stalls. They moved between eight booths, each divided by cast-iron posts, all supporting large wood beams that ran perpendicular to the aisle until coming to the building's end. At their ground level, two spacious rooms flanked the double-door entrance. The one on the left appeared to be a tack room with an assortment of work clothing, saddles, and harnesses hanging along its rustic wall. The one on the right was a utility room fitted with a water pump on its outside wall, with a collection of buckets and cleaning supplies cluttered around a massive sink. Set off to the side was a set of stairs that led to a loft.

Adam motioned. "Let's see what's up there."

The stairs groaned under their weight. They paused at the top of the small landing while Adam carefully opened the door and peered cautiously inside. The attic appeared spacious, and the moon's glow revealed it to be some type of workshop. Within the interior, an assortment of chests, some tack gear, a few blankets, a cot with a rolled-up mattress, and a bench filled its desiccated space. The accumulation of dust indicated it hadn't seen any recent use.

"At least it doesn't stink," Kyle said.

Adam unrolled the mattress. "I'll take the cot, and you can take the table."

"Why do I always get the shitty end of the stick?" squawked Kyle.

"Because I'm the brains of this here caper."

"Okay, Mr. Genius, where exactly are we?" Kyle asked mockingly.

Adam turned on his cellphone. The illumination from its screen bathed his face with a phantom-like glow that spilled into the room. "That's odd," he said while punching the screen with his index finger.

"What's odd?"

"I can't get a signal, and my phone's acting funny."

"Maybe it broke when we took a tumble?"

"Nah, it ain't broken. It just won't work."

"You may be the brains, but let me tell you something. If it won't work, it's broken."

"Shut up, grab a blanket, and take a snooze on the table. We're going to have to get up pretty early before anyone else does. I need to find my gun. I gotta hunch we're going to need it."

Kyle shook out the blanket. A cloud of dust floated in the room. He folded it several times, layering the folds into a cushion, before grabbing another blanket for protection against the night's chill. He kicked off his boots and laid down.

"Adam?"

"Yeah, what?"

"Whaddaya think those guys were doing?"

"I'm not sure. It seems they were playing with a bunch of car batteries."

"Don't you think it's a bit wonky?"

"Everything about this is wonky. Now shut up and go to sleep."

CHAPTER EIGHT

"Into the Rabbit Hole"

Adam stirred in his cot. He felt chilled by the early morning's damp air. Seeing his breath rise, he cupped his hands under the coarse wool fabric and drew it under his chin. Outside, the unmistakable drumming of rain on the roof made him dread the idea of standing in some downpour while peeing. He glanced at Kyle, who appeared to sleep peacefully without any sense of the trouble they were facing. *If we had stayed in the house, we wouldn't be in this mess. My gun, I gotta get my gun.*

"Kyle, wake up."

"What time is it?" he asked groggily.

Adam reached for his cellphone. "Something is goofy. It says nine at night."

"I told you it was broke."

Adam eyed his watch. "It's the same time as my phone."

"So what? I gotta pee," whined Kyle.

"Yeah, me, too. It's raining outside, but considering we're in some kinda stable, I think we can take a wiz with the horses."

Kyle laughed, swung out of his makeshift bed, and began to pull on his boots.

"You still got them Snickers bars?"

"Yep, right here," Kyle patted his khaki cargo pocket.

"Throw me one. I'm starving."

He tossed one to Adam.

Adam held out the crushed bar. "Nice job of flattening breakfast."

"Hey, it tastes the same."

Savagely, Adam ripped open the wrapper. With chocolate oozing down his chin, he eagerly devoured the first bite. "Damn, that's good. You got any more stuff hidden in those pockets?"

"Nope."

"C'mon, let's go downstairs," Adam ordered before wolfing down the last chunk of the chocolate bar.

The horses moved restlessly as Adam and Kyle unabashedly relieved themselves.

Among a chorus of snorts, the duo moved toward the entrance. Through a crack in the door, Adam spotted a shadowy figure walking toward them.

"Shit, someone is coming." Turning abruptly, he almost knocked over Kyle. "Quick, let's boogie upstairs."

Their hurried pace broke into a full gait as they raced to the workshop.

Back in the attic and breathing heavily, both men checked their movements.

"Now what?" Kyle asked.

"We wait."

"I'm starving."

"Me, too. Shut your yap and sit down. We gotta hang loose."

"What if he comes up here?" Kyle persisted.

"Listen, knucklehead, as long as we're quiet, he won't come up here. As soon as that guy leaves," Adam pointed toward the floor, "we'll grab something to wear to protect us from the rain, then hightail it out of here."

"Wear? Like what are we going to wear?"

"I saw some clothes in that room with all the saddles."

"Then what?"

"I find my gun, take a hike down the road, and get us some grub."

Kyle nodded. "How much dough you got?"

Adam laid down on the bare mattress. "Enough. Just relax."

From below, they heard the repetitive scraping and shuffling that went on seemingly forever. Pauses in the routine became punctuated with periods of gushing water from the squealing pump underneath their hideaway. Through this cycle of unfamiliar clatter, Adam kept playing with his cellphone, hoping to get a fix on their location. Frustrated, noting that the battery was running low, he did a hard shut down and closed his eyes.

After, what seemed to be an eternity, the routine below ended in abrupt silence.

Kyle swung off his perch on the table. "Hey, I think the guy's gone."

Adam, coming out of twilight sleep, slowly rolled off his cot and went to the door. He peeked down at the stable area and saw no movement except the horses.

"Whaddaya see?" Kyle asked.

"We have to get out of here. C'mon."

Bolting down the stairs, they turned into the tack room.

"Hey, Adam. These outfits are steampunk stuff. My sister's into this crap."

"Yeah, that's wonky. Who'd a thunk it? A place like this, having steampunk junk."

"I think this leather coat with a hood might work," said Kyle admiring it before attempting to slip it on.

"Look at me," exclaimed Adam, holding up his selection in front of him, "I got a vampire coat, but ... ."

Adam's arms halted halfway into his new-found garment. "This smells like shit."

"Yeah, mine, too," said Kyle, equally disappointed. "At least I got a hood with my army jacket."

They returned the clothing on the wall hooks.

"C'mon, let's get outta here," ordered Adam before hurrying down the corridor. Peering through the partly opened door, he saw that the coast was clear. Mentally allowing for a quick dash to the house, retrieving his gun in the gloomy predawn, and a run for the forest, Adam figured it would only take five minutes to complete. He shared his plan with Kyle.

"Now!" Adam barked before bolting toward the manor.

Surefooted in his sneakers, he outpaced Kyle, who struggled in his leather-soled boots to keep pace with him. His plan for a smooth recovery took a nose-dive when he spotted the small moat of water that surrounded the foundation. Hugging the house's base, Adam bent over, rain dripping off his cap, and combed through the swamp-like perimeter. With knees in the muck and barehanded, he frantically searched the frigid water.

"C'mon, get your ass down here and help me," Adam ordered.

Kyle stood motionless with his hands in his pockets, head bowed, and protected with the hood of his Timet. Reluctantly, he crouched down. Within a couple of minutes, he found the elusive weapon.

Kyle held it proudly in the air. "Badaboom! Here it is."

Adam snatched the firearm from Kyle's muddy hand. "No one likes a showoff."

"Hey, how about a little apprish."

"Yeah, yeah, thanks. You want a medal or something?"

Adam took the revolver and swished it in a nearby puddle, attempting to clean off some of the mud. He shoved it into the inside pocket of his peacoat. The rain began to lessen, changing into a misty sprinkle.

Rising to his full length of nearly six feet, Adam eyeballed the adjoining woods. "C'mon, follow me."

While sprinting toward the woods, both Adam and Kyle took several glances back, expecting any moment to be discovered. Stealing their way from tree to tree, they spotted a road that ran parallel to the forest. Struggling for breath, and before moving ahead, Adam began to brush the mud from his wet jeans, and Kyle followed suit.

"Damn, I'm cold, and my shoes are soaked," Adam murmured as he clumsily removed the bullets from his .38 snub-nosed revolver with his numb hands.

"What're you doing?"

"I'm trying to clean my piece."

"You gotta do that now? I'm starving,"

"Hang on to your panties. I didn't expect this gun to take a bath." Adam blew into the barrel before replacing the bullets.

"Whadda we do now?" Kyle asked.

Adam trained his eyes on the dirt road that had turned into a stream of mud. "Listen, I'm hungry, too. That road is gotta lead to somewhere—like maybe a bar or restaurant."

CHAPTER NINE

"Eightball in the Side Pocket"

Like most pool halls, Mickey's had a stratum of smoke, the smell of stale beer, and the usual collection of misfits. When Tony Angelo and Stephen entered, momentarily filling the place with much-needed sun rays, several patrons appeared to eye them with guarded curiosity. Perhaps it was the bulk of both men, Stephen's authoritarian presence, or Tony's effeminate walk that drew their attention. When the pair moved to the front counter, the curiosity eased, and the cracking of pool balls resumed, blending with the discordant music from the jukebox.

Mickey stiffened. "Mr. Angelo, what brings you here?" He faltered, "I … I mean, what can I do for you?"

Tony Angelo leaned forward on the counter while Stephen propped himself against the glass countertop with his elbows. All the clientele resumed taking a guarded interest.

"I'm looking for a couple of guys that I understand hang out in your place."

"Sure, Mr. Angelo. They have a name?"

"One's called Adam—the other's name is Kyle."

Mickey smiled. "Adam Cabano and Kyle Kroft. Sure, they come in here all the time—almost part of the furnishings. They do a lot of hustling, mostly on an unsuspecting mark."

Lowering his voice, Tony asked, "Are they in here now?"

"No, sir. Which is odd because I haven't seen them in almost three days."

"Do you know where they live?" Tony pressed.

Mickey shrugged. "Don't know for sure, somewhere on Lapham, I think."

Tony gave a sideways nod. "Do you think any of these characters know?"

"Yeah, Ramon. He's the one closest to us—the one in the red sweatshirt. I don't know if he's a buddy or not, but they shoot a lot of pool together. I've seen him leave together a few times. I'm guessing for a few beers or babes."

Tony pushed himself free of the counter and moved toward Ramon's table.

Ramon finished a power break, pocketing two striped balls when Stephen faced him, preventing any attempt to continue.

He gave Stephen a look of irritation. "You're blocking my way, Mister."

"My boss wants to have a word with you."

"Who the hell is your 'boss?'" Ramon fired back.

Stephen let his coat open slightly to reveal the Smith and Wesson 9mm pistol snugly shoulder-holstered against his massive chest. "Mr. Angelo wants to have a word with you *now*."

The "now" emphasis appeared convincing enough for Ramon to lay down his cue stick on one of the small side tables along the wall. "Hey, Carlos, hang loose. I'll be back," he said to his opponent, capping his statement with an imitative Hollywood flourish.

Tony was standing off to the side, near the front window, when Ramon swaggered up to him. "You wanna see me?" Ramon asked, his punkish demeanor fading.

Stephen crowded behind Ramon.

"Mickey tells me you're friends with a couple of guys called Adam and Kyle."

"Yeah, sort of. We shoot some pool now and then for fun." He laughed, giving the impression that it was more than fun.

Tony moved within inches of Ramon's face. "Listen, punk. I didn't call you over here so you could do your stand-up comedy routine."

Ramon's face turned ashen. He stammered, "Yeah ... yeah, we hung together. I even crashed at their place a few times."

"And where exactly is that place?"

"Eighth and Lapham."

"What's the address?" asked Tony.

"Dunno. It's not like they ever sent me a Christmas card."

"What does the building look like?"

Ramon shifted nervously in place. "Ah ... yeah, the house was brown. I think it had one of them satellite dishes on the front. Yeah, yeah, I'm sure it did."

"What else do you remember?"

Appearing panicked by the questioning, he shook his head. "Honest, Mister, I ... wait, I remember something else. There is a front door on the porch, but that's for the people downstairs. We had to use the side entrance."

Tony nodded. "Okay, get back to your game."

Turning away, Ramon almost collided with Stephen. Trying to sidestep him, Tony reached out and checked his departure by placing his beefy hand on Ramon's shoulder and spun him around.

"If you should run into either of your buddies, don't mention our little visit. *Capisce?*"

"Got it," said Ramon meekly before moving back to his game.

CHAPTER TEN

"A Person of Interest"

Captain Ed Chalmers opened his office door and scanned the collection of cubicles hoping to catch Detective Rick Morris's attention. Rather than use the inter-office phone line, he needed to stretch his legs. A shadow moved in Morris's section.

"Hey, Morris," he called out, "I need to talk with you."

Detective Morris's head popped up over his cubicle like a groundhog during mating season. With his phone pressed against his ear, he waved.

"Yeah, Captain, give me a minute," he said before ducking back into his burrow.

Chalmers turned away and left the door partially open. Returning to his desk, he eased back into his office chair, clasping his hands behind his head. He started to rhythmically rock the chair slightly while staring at the panels of the suspended ceiling.

Morris, holding the glass door, paused. "Open or closed, Captain?"

"Closed," he said, gesturing toward a chair.

Morris took a seat. "What's up?"

"I got a tip that Tony Angelo has been making some interesting calls lately."

"Like what?"

"Like he's been taking an interest in a couple of small-time operators. You know, hustlers who think they can break into the big time."

"What're their names?"

"Adam Cabano and Kyle Kroft."

"Doesn't ring any bells."

"They're a couple of low-life with rap sheets that wouldn't draw any interest from the Milwaukee Mob. Sure, they aren't saints, but they aren't what you would call *made men*."

"Okay, what's all the fuss about?"

"Tony's been a pain in my ass ever since I took this job. He's one clever bastard. Rumor has it he's responsible for a lot of hit jobs."

"You're not telling me anything I don't know, Captain."

"Yeah, yeah, I'm only blowing off steam. Anyway, I was wondering why Tony is taking an interest in these two bums."

"Maybe they tried to hustle Tony."

Captain Chalmers shook his head. "If so, they're not the sharpest crayons in the box. If they tried any shit like that, they're living on borrowed time. Rumor has it, Lake Michigan's full of Tony's enemies."

"Yeah, I heard it referred to as Tony's locker. Okay, so what's my role in this?"

"I'm glad you asked," the captain said with a wry smile.

"These two schmucks may be our key to locking up Angelo once and for all."

"Here's the thing," Captain Chalmers began. "Tony never does his own dirty work. He's too smart for that. Whatever these guys did to ruffle his feathers, he's taking a personal interest in them and letting down his guard. This ... whatever it is, vendetta or just raw revenge, makes him vulnerable. And we're going to take advantage of it."

"And how do I fit into the plan?"

"You've been working on the Stys case. I want you to hand it off to Edwards."

"Okay. Am I going to get any help or backup on this?"

Captain Chalmers rose from his chair and pointed toward the map of Milwaukee, sectioned off by district. "Here's the thing," he began with his usual introductory phrase, "Tony's territory pretty much includes District 2 and 6." He waved his hand over them.

"So?"

"You're an honest cop. That's why I've selected you for this assignment."

"Okay ... ?" said Morris, his reply drawn out more like a question.

"Internal Affairs has been looking into the activity of several of the cops in those two districts. It seems they get favors from Tony. And Tony gets favors in return."

"So, you're afraid of a leak?"

"Yeah, I'm sorry to say. This lead is too good to take a chance that Tony Angelo will get wind of our interest."

"Okay, but he knows we're always interested in anything he does, and you never answered my question about help with this."

Captain Chalmers returned to his seat. "We're getting a rookie into homicide. She starts today."

"Her?"

"Yeah, her," the captain fired back. "Susan Dunlap rated high at the academy and hasn't been contaminated by the system. She's single, doesn't have a boyfriend, and is eager to take on a challenge."

"No boyfriend. She must be a dog."

"Hey, you're no Christian Bale yourself. So, you two should get along quite well. The fact that you're not attached lessens other problems if you know what I mean. But of course, that can lead to other problems. So, keep it in your pants."

"How do you know I'm not seeing someone?"

Chalmers laughed. "Call it police intuition. If you were seeing someone, you'd be bragging up a storm and have her picture on your desk. So, it's elementary, Detective Morris."

Morris forced a laugh, crossed his arms over his chest, and shifted in place. "Okay, I got a partner. When do I meet her?"

"Right now," he said before coaxing someone on the outside of his office to enter.

When the door opened, Morris shot to his feet. His attention appeared focused on an attractive brunette, about 5'8", with her hair formed into a tight military-style bun and wearing a Milwaukee police officer's uniform. She extended her hand to Captain Chalmers. "Officer Susan Dunlap, reporting for duty, sir."

Chalmers accepted the handshake. "Relax. We're not big on formal protocols."

She withdrew her hand. "Yes, sir," she said and assumed a parade rest position.

"Officer Dunlap, I'd like you to meet Detective Rick Morris. He'll be your partner for this assignment."

She turned and accepted Morris's hand. "Pleased to meet you, Detective Morris."

"Likewise."

"Officer Dunlap, have a seat," commanded Captain Chalmers.

With his eyes still fixed on Dunlap, Morris eased back down into his seat.

"Here's the thing," Chalmers began. "You two will be shadowing Tony Angelo. Your cover will be as a married couple. You'll wear regular street clothes and drive your own cars. Keep track of your mileage for reimbursement as well as all meals."

"Hey, Captain," Morris chimed in. "Are you saying that if Tony goes into the Pfister, we gotta follow him, and the meal is on Milwaukee Police Department?"

Captain Chalmers shot Morris a look. "No, smartass. Exercise some common sense. That's why I have you teamed up with Officer Dunlap."

Morris turned a shade of red, and Dunlap snickered.

"Okay. Now, getting back to Tony. He's got a peculiar interest in two guys—Adam Cabano and Kyle Kroft. They're a couple of small-time felons, and that's what makes this so interesting. Your assignment is finding out why."

"Captain, how did you get the lead on Tony's interest in the first place?" asked Morris, who's red coloring began to fade.

"Our informant, who runs the pool hall on First and Mitchell."

"Sir, when do we start?" asked Dunlap.

"As soon as you get into your undercover work clothes."

CHAPTER ELEVEN

"Do You Want Fries with That?"

Adam was the first to enter the Green Hog, ducking a bit to avoid hitting his head on a low-hanging timber. The pub's interior, lit by candlelight and supplemented with oil lamps, suggested a dive. The fireplace offered additional illumination, but it was the warmth that drew Adam and Kyle to its hearth. The pub had a collection of queer-looking patrons who carefully studied them as they moved toward the heat.

Adam draped his wet peacoat over the back of the chair. Kyle followed suit and removed his rain-soaked army fatigue jacket, shaking it slightly before placing it on his chair. Adam's chambray shirt was damp around the collar, while Kyle's black, printed hoodie sweatshirt proclaiming, "Ahoy ladies," appeared dry.

A barmaid, with hair curled into an unkempt mass together with a few ringlets adorning her temples, moved assertively to their table. She wore a long, full-style dress with puffed shoulders and a plunging bodice.

"What can I get for you two gentlemen?" she asked warmly.

"A couple of burgers and some beer," replied Adam, who was rubbing his hands near the fire.

"Ah, a pair of Yankees," she said, placing her hands on her waistline, with fingers wedged into her white apron strings.

There was a flurry of laughter among the other patrons.

Adam scrutinized their fellow diners.

The barmaid, smiling her amusement, said, "I can fetch the beer, but I fear we don't have what you call a 'burger'"

"Then, what do you have to eat?" asked Adam.

"Gentlemen, I fear all we have today is porkpie."

"Okay, we'll have the porkpie and two Millers."

More laughter.

"Sir, the closest miller is nearly ten kilometers away. That M on your cap, are you a miller?"

"No," snapped Adam, "that's for the Milwaukee Brewers baseball team."

"Baseball?"

"Yeah, the Brewers ... in Milwaukee. Didn't you ever hear of them?" asked Adam, beginning to feel embarrassed by the questioning.

"No," said the waitress, her smile growing.

"Never mind," snapped Adam. "Just give us that porkpie and any brand of beer you got. And ain't you got any electricity in this place?"

"Electricity?"

"Yeah, you know, electricity for your light bulbs."

"Light bulbs? No, Sir," the waitress replied before leaving.

Kyle leaned over to Adam. "There's something goofy about this place.

"Like, totally nutso."

The waitress, still wearing a sheepish smile, dropped off two tankards of beer and left.

Adam and Kyle eagerly grabbed the drinks and took a gulp.

"This stuff's warm as piss," scoffed Kyle, wiping his face with his shirt sleeve.

"Maybe their refrigerator's on the fritz, along with the lights?"

commented Adam, removing the beer off his upper lip with the back of his hand.

After a brief wait, their beer half consumed, the waitress reappeared, clutching two metal plates, each holding a serving of food.

Adam asked, "What's the name of this burg?"

"Burg?"

"Yeah, what do you call this place?"

"Boldon New Winning," she said briskly before leaving, her smile evaporating as quickly as she left.

"I ain't never heard of a place called Boldon ... whatever," Adam muttered.

Eyeing his meal, he cautiously prodded the pie with his fork. He watched Kyle do the same, then observed the other patrons continuing to take an unusual interest in them.

The pair quickly consumed their meal, leaving only crumbs on their plates as they held their tankards in the air.

"A couple more beers!" Kyle yelled.

The waitress brought a large pitcher to the table, "Gentlemen, what manner of costume is your attire?" she asked while filling their mugs. "I've never seen anyone garbed like you before."

"Our threads? This is how we dress in Milwaukee," Adam answered.

"I've seen a few Yankees when I visited London," the waitress began, "mostly sailors, but they certainly were not clothed like you two gentlemen."

"Well, the people in Milwaukee do," Adam scoffed before drawing the mug of beer to his lips.

Taking her pitcher of beer, she moved to another table.

Adam drew closer to Kyle. "Did you notice, everyone is paying in pool change?" he whispered covertly.

"I got a pocket full of case quarters, leftover from our last game," Kyle said.

"I'll call the hottress over and ask how much this foodoo costs."

Adam waved.

When the waitress approached their table, she appeared more restrained. "Yes, sir."

"What do we owe for the food and beer?"

"That'll be a shilling, sir—plus me tip," she said, her smile returning.

"Shilling? What country are we in?"

She gave both a curious stare. "By the manner of your speech and your most peculiar queries, I most certainly imagine you two to have escaped from a lunatic asylum," she said jestingly. "You are most certainly playing some type of a joke on me, for you must know you are in England."

Shocked by her disclosure, yet feeling the sting of the insult, he retorted, "We are as sane as you, lady."

Her smile wavered as she began to turn to leave.

Adam raised his hand like a schoolboy in class. "One more question. What's today's date?"

She paused, her eyebrows rising. "Are yea certain you haven't received a blow to your 'ead? Why this is the second of October of 1854, in the year of our good Queen Victoria."

Adam stared at Kyle in disbelief.

When she left, Adam glanced at a nearby table, eyeing the coinage left behind.

"Put two of your quarters on the table," Adam ordered, then pointed at the adjacent table. "It's about the same size as those coins. We got to haul ass."

"But, I gotta piss," Kyle balked.

"Piss outside. Let's go."

CHAPTER TWELVE

"The Crib"

Detective Rick Morris blew into the small opening of his Styrofoam cup, attempting to cool his coffee, while Officer Susan Dunlap munched on her granola bar.

"Yah know, the more coffee you drink, the more you're going to need a bathroom," Officer Dunlap said between bites.

"The more of them high fiber bars you eat, the more you'll be needing a bathroom, too," retorted Morris.

An uneasy silence descended in the vehicle, interrupted by an awkward symphony of crunches and slurps.

"So, the captain tells me you're an Afghanistan War veteran."

"Yes, sir," Officer Dunlap answered crisply.

"We're going to be doing this stakeout stuff for quite a while, so you can cut the *Sir* stuff."

"Yes, sir. I mean, okay." She crushed the bar wrapper and put it into the cup holder.

"Hey, we can stay on a first name basis while we're on this assignment."

"Okay, but after all my training, it'll be a change," she said.

"What did you do when you were there?"

"I was a communications officer, working in the TOC."

"TOC?"

"The Tactical Operations Center—TOC for short."

"So, you were an officer. What was your rank?" Morris asked, keeping his attention focused on Adam and Kyle's place, two blocks away.

"Captain."

"Wow, isn't this a step-down?"

"It all depends on how you look at it."

"How's that?"

"The next step for me would be major, and that required two more years as captain."

Morris took a long sip of coffee. "How many years did you have in?"

"Eight."

"Couldn't take two more years of military life?"

"It wasn't that. I had a boyfriend," Dunlap said, her voice quaking.

"A bad breakup, huh?"

"Not exactly. Tim was a captain and sapper."

Morris glanced at Dunlap. "What's a sapper?"

"Sappers support units on the front line. They do everything from communications, logistics, route clearance to building roads and bridges. That's how we met."

"So, Susan, I'm guessing Tim wasn't so lucky in clearing the route."

Dunlap glared at him. "Maybe we should stick to sir and officer."

"Hey, I'm sorry," Morris said after an uneasy silence. "You lose sensitivity after a while in this job."

She returned to staring forward out the car's window. "To your question, Tim was shot in the back by an Afghan soldier. The coward killed three more of our troops before being neutralized."

Detective Morris drank more freely while surveying Lapham Street.

"Well, Mr. Foot-in-the-mouth, what's your story?" asked Dunlap.

"I've been on the force ten years."

"That's not much of a story. Fill in the blanks."

"I was married once. I don't think she liked being a cop's wife."

"This *she,* she got a name?"

"Patty."

"That's it?"

"Yep, pretty much."

"You don't think your lack of sympathy had anything to do with it?" Dunlap asked, then chortled.

"You know how to hurt a guy."

She smiled. "Maybe I'm already learning from the master."

Morris returned the smile and glanced at his watch. "Ten. I think we'll give this a couple more hours than call it a night."

"Okay, but what exactly are we doing here, besides keeping tabs on Adam and Kyle's place?"

"Tony Angelo has been untouchable for years. For some reason, he's taken a personal interest in these two guys. Right now, we're using them as bait and seeing why this particular piece of cheese has caught the interest of Tony the Rat."

"So, we're not sure what this is all about."

"Yep, and you should be honored to be a part of this."

"How so?" she asked.

"Well, you're a rookie, and rookies usually get the shit jobs. We are going after a Mob kingpin. That's something beginners typically don't do. Someone at the top must like you."

"Maybe this is a shit job because I don't have any relatives in high places."

"Maybe it's your karma."

"You mean being stuck with you?"

"Ha, ha. You really are a quick learner."

They both laughed.

CHAPTER THIRTEEN

"Hey, Buddy, Can You Spare Me a Sixpence?"

Adam and Kyle shot out of the Green Hog and made a path straight for the nearest stand of trees. The rain was gone, but the ground was soaked, making it difficult for them to travel. A leftover blanket of clouds hid the moon's radiance, providing cover for their dine-and-dash escape.

"Phew, that was close," gasped Adam as he leaned on a tree for support.

"Yeah, too close for comfort," Kyle agreed as he relieved himself into a nearby bush.

Adam moved away, choosing another direction.

Having taken care of their immediate needs, they found a fallen trunk and sat on its damp surface.

"Now what?" asked Kyle.

"We gotta get some money," Adam promptly replied.

"How do we do that? Stick up a bank?"

"That's not a bad idea, but we have to find a bank first. I don't recall seeing any, so we need to find something else."

"How about a gas station?"

"Hey, moron, they didn't have gas stations in 1854."

"Oh."

"But they did have churches, and churches have lots of dough."

"Yeah, and we did pass one on the way here," Kyle said, a smile growing on his face.

———

Partially obscured by the evening's fog, St. Nicholas Church's outline appeared, identified only by the signage adjacent to its entry road. The parish grounds, situated on a hill and almost entirely encircled by a graveyard, proved to be a challenge as Adam and Kyle weaved their way through an adjoining stand of trees. Mindful that their presence, if discovered, would pose a problem at this late hour, they cautiously sloshed through the soggy grounds, interspersed with fragments of quarried stone.

"How are we gonna get in there?" asked Kyle, trailing closely behind Adam.

"You forget, I'm the best lock-breaker in the business."

"Then how come you used the bolt cutter to get the chair?"

"There is the easy way and the hard way. The bolt cutter was the easy way at the time," Adam said.

"Well, ya ain't got cutters on this caper."

"So, we do it the hard way."

Shrouded in darkness, Adam and Kyle peered around the side of the church and eyed the nearby parsonage. The warm glow of a candle danced in a window frame—evidence of occupancy. Slinking around the corner, Adam felt for the church's door handle and lock. "It's a lever lock," he whispered before drawing back into the shadows.

"Can you crack it?" asked Kyle.

"A piece of cake. It's a curtain lever lock."

He pulled out a small case from the inside pocket of his peacoat. "I want you to stay right here. It's a one-man job. Just keep your yap shut and your eyes open."

Adam once more approached the door, and with blind dexterity, felt for the keyhole. Taking a filed down key, he joined a lever-picking tool to it and inserted both pieces into the keyway. Twisting the pick until he heard a click, Adam moved to the next lever until each was undone. Finished, he removed the pick and applied pressure with the key nub until he retracted the bolt.

"Kyle, get over here," he whispered.

The door to the church groaned as they entered.

"You still have that flashlight, don't you?" asked Adam.

Kyle patted his jacket pocket. "Yeah, right here."

"Turn it on."

The beam shot forward, hitting the altar, producing a radiance that caused the entire church's interior to glow.

"Hey, shithead, I want to see not let everyone in this village know we're here."

Kyle cupped his hand over the lens, letting only a sliver of light escape from the openings in his fist.

"Move it to the left," commanded Adam.

Using the cupped flashlight, with its reddish glow, they followed the pale light to a closed door. Adam tried the doorknob and found it to be unlocked. The room appeared to be an office with only one window. From outside, the fog-shrouded moon offered little illumination. The desk, situated on the far end of the room, was more of a cupboard fixed firmly to the wall. On each side of the cabinet, two doors secured with locks begged exploration.

Standing before the door on the right, Adam dropped to his knees and retrieved his lock picker's kit once more. "These are easy ones," he said, placing an L-shaped tool into the keyway. Without the finesse used on the entryway, he randomly twisted the device until the lock snapped open. "Like I said, easy as light cheese."

Peering inside, Adam reached in and pulled out a small strongbox. Although plain-looking, except for its decorative handle, it did not yield when he tried to open it.

"Shit," Adam exclaimed. He shook it. The sound of possible

coinage provided an incentive to continue. "There better be something worthwhile inside."

The lock, a barrel-hole keyway, Adam applied the same procedures he used to gain entry to the church. "Now, let's see what treasure we have found," he said, lifting the lid.

Kyle aimed his flashlight inside the box. Paper money and coins covered the bottom. He picked up a handful. "What kind of money is this?"

"Hell if I know, and cover that light," snapped Adam. "It's dough, and that's all we need to know. We gotta get out of here. Grab it, and let's scram."

After emptying the box and stuffing the spoils into their pockets, they retraced their steps. Moving toward the back of the church, they froze. In the doorway, a man blocked their path. He held a lamp high over his head and squinted into the interior.

"Oy, what have we 'ere?" the man said, brandishing a club in his free hand.

Kyle trained his flashlight on the man's face.

The man drew back and shielded his face with his club-wielding arm. He yelled, "A couple of cracksmen are ye?"

Then, using the club to sound the alarm, he began to bang loudly on the church door like a drum. "Thieves! Thieves!"

The repeated cries unnerved Adam. He drew his revolver, pointed it, and pulled the trigger.

CHAPTER FOURTEEN

"On Point"

Detective Rick Morris glanced at his watch, yawned, and tried to stretch in the limited confines of his Subaru Forester. "It's almost midnight. I want to get home before I turn into a pumpkin."

Officer Susan Dunlap moved the binoculars to her eyes. "A black Mercedes isn't the kind of vehicle that fits in this neighborhood," she said, fixing her gaze on the new arrival.

"Lemme have a look." Morris reached out.

Dunlap relinquished the glasses and stiffened to attention.

"Well, well," he began, "like I always said, hoodlums and rats come out at night."

They both watched as the car came to a stop in front of Adam Cabano and Kyle Kroft's duplex. The lights from the Mercedes died.

Morris rested his elbows on the steering wheel, using it to steady the binoculars in his hands.

After a moment of silence, Dunlap asked, "What's happening?"

"Nothing. They're only sitting in the car. Maybe they're waiting for Adam and Kyle to show up. It's nearly midnight, and the bars close at two. This stakeout just got longer."

"Is it Tony?" she asked.

"It's too hard for me to tell from this distance. I'm assuming it's him and his driver, Stephen. We're going to hafta wait this out."

"You know his driver's name?"

"Stephen's been with him for years. I think he's the only one Tony trusts."

It wasn't too long after Morris spoke when the vehicle's dome light went on, and the driver exited.

The man walked to the house and disappeared down the side driveway. After a few minutes, he returned to the Mercedes. With equal swiftness, the lights on their car came on, and it raced away.

Morris and Dunlap ducked under the dash.

Before starting the engine, Detective Morris made sure the coast was clear.

"Why do you think they left in such a hurry?" asked Officer Dunlap.

"Maybe they told him they already bought Girl Scout cookies at the office."

"Am I going to be treated to your jokes during this operation?"

"Yep. Consider it a bonus."

"Yippee, skippy," she muttered.

"Let's go see why he left in such a hurry."

"I thought the plan was to keep Tony in our sights when we had a chance?" Dunlap said.

"It's late. Tony is probably heading home to Waukesha. I'm more interested in why the visit was so short."

Morris brought the Subaru to a stop across the street from the duplex and killed the lights. "I'm going to check it out. I'll keep the engine running in case we hafta haul butt."

Detective Morris got out of his car and glanced up at the top floor of the duplex. All the window coverings were drawn, and not so much as a speck of light hinted of occupancy. The front window on the lower floor danced with the glow from a television. In the driveway, parked in front of the garage, stood a green Ford Ranger. Behind the Ranger, nearly touching the front sidewalk, a beat-up gray Cadillac was parked inches from the Ford's rear bumper.

Detective Morris climbed the steps of the side porch. Noting the mailbox was full, he pulled out its contents. Fanning the collection of junk mail, he spotted a few notices from credit card companies. After shoving the mail back, he opened the storm door to see if any message may have been tucked between the doorjamb. Once more, nothing.

As he began to descend the side porch, the front door opened. A man wearing a white athletic shirt and brown pajama bottoms confronted him while holding a Louisville Slugger.

"Why the hell you poking around here so late at night?" he asked, extending the bat toward Morris.

"I'm looking for Adam Cabano."

"Kinda late to be visiting, don't you think?" he said and moved closer to the porch's railing.

"I'm a friend of Adam's. I work second shift and couldn't get here earlier."

"I'm not so sure you're telling me the truth. You don't look like the kind of guy that hangs out with him."

"We're not that close."

The man in the pajama bottoms drew closer. "You're some kind of bill collector, aren't you? You're the second guy that's been here in less than fifteen minutes."

"I don't know anything about that," Morris said matter-of-factly.

"Well, he hasn't been around here in three days."

"Yeah, I've been trying to contact him in as many days, too."

"Well, if you see him before I do, tell him I'm calling a towing service for his truck. We have an agreement. I let him park his piece-of-shit in my driveway, so he doesn't have to pay for a street parking permit. The agreement is he moves it every morning so that I can get in and out of my garage."

"Yeah, if I see him first, I'll let him know you're pissed. I gotta go," Morris said. He turned and began to walk toward the street.

"Hey, Mister," the man called out.

"Yeah?"

"When I do see him, you got a name so I can tell him who stopped by?"

"No, but you can tell him to watch his back."

CHAPTER FIFTEEN

"Drake's Drum"

The wetness of the forest drenched Adam and Kyle as they pushed their way through its protective foliage. With only the moon's faint glow as their guide, they received random buffets from low-hung boughs that snapped in their faces.

Kyle, gasping for breath, waited until he was deep inside the woods before turning on his flashlight.

"Shit, we're so screwed," exclaimed Adam before collapsing on the damp ground.

Kyle aimed the beam at Adam, who had buried his face into his hands.

"Shut that damn thing off."

"Okay, okay, don't snap my head off. Whaddaya we gonna do now?"

"Hop off, man. If that guard, or whatever he was, hadn't shown up, we'd be home free. I didn't mean to kill him. Shit, I never offed anyone," Adam sobbed. Rising quickly, he hurriedly went a few steps into the thicket and began to throw up. Purging himself of his meal, Adam wiped his soiled face with the back of his hand. With shaky knees, he returned and beheld the fear and uncertainty written on Kyle's face.

"Can't we just go back to that *Addams Family* place and book it?" Kyle asked, his voice pleading.

Adam checked himself. "Okay, genius, do you have any idea where we are? Because I don't."

Silent except for his labored breathing, Kyle leaned against a nearby tree.

"Maybe you're right," Adam finally said. "We went straight into this elf-looking neighborhood, so all we have to do is backspace."

"Won't people be looking for someone who whacked that guy?"

"Yeah. If we really did a backflip in history, do you know what they did to murderers back then in England?"

"Hang 'um?"

"That ain't the half of it. They hung 'um, cut out their guts, and then attach four horses to their arms and legs and make them pull you apart."

"Shit," Kyle muttered, "ain't that, unconstipational?"

"You're out to lunch. We ain't in Kansas anymore, Einstein."

"So, what are we gonna do now?"

"We only have one choice. We don't have to go back all the way, just close enough to find that road we followed into town. It's a simple plan," Adam said, rising from the ground. "C'mon, let's boogie."

When Adam and Kyle approached the road, they recognized the area as having been previously traveled on their way into town. Staying close to the protective cover of the forest, they remained within sight of the road. Nearing the halfway mark, they heard the thunder of an approaching rider. Going deeper into the woods, they noted the rider racing in the same direction as they were traveling. Once the lone horseman had galloped past, they moved closer to the road and continued on their journey.

Adam and Kyle arrived damp and exhausted. The moon, having set, slowly surrendered its feeble light to the advancing glow of dawn. They momentarily stood in the tree line, gazing at the seemingly deserted estate through the mist-covered landscape, and considered their next move.

"I think the sun is gonna be coming up pretty soon," said Adam. "And we hafta make it into that barn before it does. Before we try to break into that house, I gotta get some sleep. I'm beat."

Sprinting from the thicket, they charged through the predawn fog into the stable then up the stairs to their sanctuary. Sapped of energy, Adam and Kyle resumed their former resting places. They quickly fell asleep without a word between them, never troubling to remove their clothing or footwear.

———

Dragged off his cot, Adam thought his arms would be pulled from their sockets as he hit the floor. Unsure of his attackers, he struggled to gain a footing as a coarse bag slipped over his head.

"Get that damn bag off of me," he yelled, involuntarily sucking in pieces of fabric and dust. He spat out its loose vestiges and tried to breathe at the same time. Someone punched him in his gut. He gasped for air, inhaling more specks of something unpleasant. Through the mesh of the rough cloth, he detected Kyle's silhouette as he, too, was caught in his own struggle. With arms flaying about, he heard him unleash a torrent of profanities on his attackers.

"Well, we've got us a feisty one here, me lads," someone said.

"He's got quite a blooming tongue," one of the men shouted.

"This will cure 'em," another man cried before Adam heard Kyle howl in pain and drop to the floor.

As the attention partially shifted away from him, Adam broke free from his captor, tore off his head covering, and dove toward his cot. He reached for his pistol, which he had hidden under the mattress. Before he could bring it to bear, his arm received a blow from a baton. The gun fell to the floor with a thud.

The man wielding the club picked up the .38 revolver and held it high. "Here it is, lads," he exclaimed. "It's the barking iron which done in poor ol' Silas. Blimey, we got us our cracksmen, by jiminy."

Those were the last words Adam heard before being struck on the head.

CHAPTER SIXTEEN

"In for a Penny, in for a Pound"

Adam slowly came to and rubbed the bump on his head. His head throbbed as he stroked his wet hair. Drawing his manacled hands in front of him, he saw they were blood-stained. Adam sensed the room move and then realized it wasn't a room but a wagon's interior. With his hands and feet in shackles, he watched the open window, covered with crossbars, appear to dance while the carriage moved to an unknown destination. He felt queasy.

"Welcome to earth," Kyle said as he remained curled into a ball at the rear of the wagon.

"How long have I been out?"

"Not sure. Maybe you were in la-la land for half an hour. The bastards jacked all of our stuff, 'cept our clothes and caps. They got your blah-blah box."

"What about your flashlight?"

"They didn't take it cuz I stashed it on one of the shelves before I hit the sack."

Adam checked all his pockets. When he reached the inner one, he smiled. After removing his hand, he patted his breast. "They didn't get my skeleton key."

"One of the dudes said they're going to hang us for murder."

Adam rubbed the back of his neck with his right hand, the shackle's cold chain chafing his throat. "Not if we can get back to that flying DeLorean."

"You know, Adam, that chair doesn't really fly," Kyle said.

"What are you talking about?"

"I mean, the chair doesn't move. Only whatever sits in it does."

"So what? It's gonna get us out of this hellhole."

"I was just saying," Kyle replied.

The wagon came to a stop. The door swung open, hitting the side of the wagon with a thud. Three men, each carrying a truncheon, stood at the ready. Grinning, they repeatedly struck their open palms with the clubs menacingly.

One of the men gestured to the two of them to come down. "Step lively, lads. We got ye a nice salt box for you to rest in before the hanging."

All three laughed.

"I want a lawyer," demanded Kyle as he jumped down.

"You'll have to speak to the magistrate, *Your Highness*," the guard, holding a lantern, mocked and prodded him forward.

Adam, flanked by the last two men, shuffled forward, his steps checked by the limits of his ankle chains.

"Here ye are lads, your royal chamber," said the tallest of the three men, his remark laced with mockery.

Forced through a narrow doorway, Adam and Kyle cautiously moved into the darkness. The door behind them closed with ominous finality. Like a couple of mimes, they ran their hands over the damp brick walls, blindly exploring their new residence until bumping into each other.

"Hey, man, watch it," said Adam.

"Sorry, this place is darker than black."

Silently, they withdrew from the center of the cell. Kyle and Adam sat on opposing bunks, finding their accommodations nothing more than foul-smelling wood planks secured to the walls with lengths of chain.

"Now what?" asked Kyle.

"It's a triple stumper. All this shit is pissing me off. Shouldn't we have a shit sucker?"

"Those guys laughed when I asked for a lawyer."

Adam cleared his throat. "Maybe we'll see 'im tomorrow."

"I don't want to be, what you said before, pulled apart by horses."

"Hanged, drawn, and quartered. That's what they called it back then ... I mean now."

Adam heard soft whimpering. "Don't be a wahface. We aren't standing on them galluses yet. Try to get some shuteye."

———

Kyle sat on his bunk, his face cradled in his hands, and looked at Adam, who appeared to be in deep thought. He lowered his hands and rested them on his knees. "Whaddaya thinking?" he asked.

Adam shifted his gaze to Kyle. "I'm thinking we're stuck in this shit-hole, and I ain't got any idea how we're gonna get out of Dodge." He turned away.

"C'mon, dude, yah gotta have a plan," Kyle begged. "I'm not ready to hang with Elvis."

"Unless God comes back from lunch and saves our asses, we're gonna be staying rent-free on death row for a while."

There was a clang of metal before the door swung open. One of the men from the night before stood in the doorway, carrying two metal plates. Behind him, another man, broad-shouldered and appearing bad-tempered, stood holding a ring of keys. The man with the dishes moved in slightly before placing them on the floor. "Here's your food. Eat up, lads. You're in luck. The circuit judge will be 'earing your case today at noon." He turned and secured the door once more.

Kyle, his chains rattling, moved to pick up the plates. He sniffed one of the dishes before handing the other to Adam. "What do you think this stuff is?"

"Food," Adam said indifferently, grabbed a rust-pocked spoon, and began to wolf down his meal.

CHAPTER SEVENTEEN

"Rub-a-Dub-Dub"

Officer Susan Dunlap yawned as she slid into the passenger side of Detective Rick Morris's Subaru.

"You can't be tired," he joked, "you had at least six hours of sleep."

"After my shower and putting on my face, more like five."

"Well, I'm raring to go," he chirped.

"That's easy for you guys. All you need is a splash of water on your face, Old Spice in your armpits, and a change of underwear, and you're all set." She sniffed the air. "You did change your underwear, didn't you?"

"Very funny. During your morning routine, did you have a chance to eat?"

"No."

"I figured as much, so I got us a couple of crullers and coffee." He reached behind the seat and retrieved two white paper bags. He handed one to Dunlap. "After last night, I wasn't sure if you drank coffee."

"Yeah, I drink coffee, but not at midnight." She accepted the offering. "Thanks. Where are we off to?"

Morris placed his coffee in the holder, removed the cruller from the bag, and took a large bite. "Tony usually begins his day at the office."

"Office? Tony Angelo has an office?" Dunlap took a sip of her drink.

Detective Morris pulled away from the curb and merged with the early morning traffic. "Yep. Tony's got an office in one of his laundromats. This one's located in West Allis."

"Isn't that out of our jurisdiction?"

"Yeah, so what? Tony has his favorite hangouts, and his interests don't stop at the city limits. And neither should ours. The County Sheriff has his hands full between their Criminal Investigations Division, General Investigations Unit, and the Apprehension Unit. So, I won't be stepping on anyone's toes."

"Do they know what we're up to?"

"Every police department in Milwaukee County would like a piece of Tony. Our job is to find out why Tony, the Cat, is interested in Adam Cabano and Kyle Kroft."

"Tony, the Cat?"

Morris finished the last bite of his cruller and licked his fingers before grabbing a napkin from the bag. "Yeah. It's kind of a joke. See, Tony has an unusual walk. He kinda walks a little light in the loafers."

"You mean he's gay?"

"Not hardly. Tony hates the label, and no one calls him that to his face. His walk makes him appear effeminate. That can give some people the wrong impression that he's a pussy. Trust me—he's a cold-blooded killer. The trouble is, he hasn't been caught in the act or finked on by any of his associates."

"What makes Captain Chalmers so interested in Adam and Kyle?"

"Tony always has his dirty work done by other people. We know that for certain. Once, we got someone to rat on him. Tony's men got to him before it went to trial. He just disappeared. No body, no witness. That turned out to be good advertising for anyone who thought about singing."

"You're not answering my question."

"As I said, Tony likes to delegate. This is the first time he has taken a personal interest in these two guys—or anyone for that matter. So, the Captain thinks Tony's going to get his hands dirty on this one.

"And?"

"And, we are the ones who will bring him in. Score one for the Milwaukee Police Department." He made an imaginary check in the air.

"Okay, sounds good and all that, but what about the FBI? Don't you think they're interested, too?" asked Dunlap.

"I'm sure they are, but I don't think those college boys and girls from Quantico understand the significance of what's going on. Those two unfortunate bums did something to Tony for him to break his rule of involvement."

Detective Morris guided his Subaru into the far end of the parking lot, picking a spot sheltered from plain view. Across the street, the *Suds Your Duds Laundromat and Dry Cleaners* appeared busy. A couple of the company's delivery trucks were backed into the loading dock and were in the process of being filled.

"I don't see Tony's black Mercedes," said Dunlap, still nursing her coffee.

"I tailed him before," remarked Morris. "He's a late riser. Don't worry. He'll be here."

"What makes you so sure?"

"He's a creature of habit."

Dunlap set her cup in the center column's rest. "When I was in the military, whenever we went outside the wire, we had to change our schedules and routes so the enemy couldn't predict our movements."

"I agree, but Tony does his own thing. He has this obsession with routine. I guess, so far, he hasn't had to worry about it. That kind of routine gives him a solid alibi when someone gets whacked."

"Okay, I understand, but isn't it dangerous for him to be changing his MO?"

"Yes, it is, and we are going to find out why. Just sit back and relax."

Morris, taking his own advice, slumped back into his seat. "Let me know when you see Tony's car," he said before closing his eyes.

"Considering I had but five hours of sleep, shouldn't I be the one taking a nap?" asked Dunlap.

"You were in the military. Didn't you learn that rank has its privileges?"

Before Morris could nod off, a black Mercedes pulled into the parking lot across the street. Tony's driver exited the vehicle and then held the door open for his boss. Their swiftness indicated urgency as they entered the building.

"Sorry to wake you from your slumber, but Tony has arrived." Her voice had a lilt in it as if she took pleasure in the interruption.

Morris, his eyes shut, said matter-of-factly, "Good. Let me know if he starts to leave."

"Ah, the way they're moving tells me they're up to something."

"What do you mean?" he said, pulling himself upright.

"They are moving way too fast for an average day at the office."

Although the binoculars were not necessary, Detective Morris retrieved them from the back seat. As he was about to use them, he caught sight of Tony and his driver leaving the building. "I see what you mean." He handed the glasses to Dunlap.

"I guess your little nap wasn't in the cards," she said before training the glasses on the two men.

Morris started the engine. "That's okay. It's what I live for—the chase."

CHAPTER EIGHTEEN

"The Magistrate"

Adam and Kyle stood on a raised platform in the center of the magistrate's office. They shifted uneasily as their chains rattled against the three-sided cast-iron railing enclosure. Downcast, they avoided the stares of the unruly onlookers who managed to press around the walls of the smoke-filled room. Some of the spectators who were unable to gain entry succeeded in securing a vantage point outside the courtroom's few windows. A festival-like atmosphere permeated the assembly.

From their perch, the local justice of the peace and traveling magistrate looked down with noticeable contempt on the two men. The bailiff, dressed in his uniform with keys secured to the front of his belt, appeared poised for guidance from the official. Below the magistrate's bench, two men dressed in more formal attire began conversing with each other.

"These proceedings will come to order," the justice of the peace yelled over the noise. The clatter diminished except for the muted rumblings of a few.

"Adam Cabano and Kyle Kroft," began the magistrate, his eyebrows raised in outward puzzlement, "you are being charged in this petty court for the wanton murder of Phineas Hogwood, the town's night watchman."

"We didn't kill him!" exclaimed Adam.

"The accused will remain silent," ordered the justice of the peace.

A wave of palpable excitement swept through the gathering.

"Are there any witnesses against these men?" bellowed the magistrate.

A smartly dressed man sitting below the court officers rose. "We call Lord Byron Turner."

A short, plump man squeezed his way through a cluster of people. He removed his hat and stood before the witness stand.

"Lord Turner, do you swear and affirm that the testimony you are about to give is the truth, so help you, God?" asked the magistrate.

"I do so affirm."

"Lord Turner, do you know these men?"

"Yes, Your Lordship. These are the men who hid in my stable and took over its workshop."

The magistrate held up Adam's .38 snub-nose revolver. "Do you recognize this unusual weapon?"

"Yes, Your Lordship. It was that man's weapon," he pointed at Adam. "I was informed, he tried to use it against the constable and his men when they came to arrest them. I was outside the stable as they were being led away."

"It's not mine. I found it on the road," Adam yelled over the uncontrolled anger that swelled throughout the room.

"The accused will remain silent," the magistrate shouted. "You will have your opportunity to speak."

"Lord Turner, you may step down," the Justice of the Peace said.

Again, the barrister rose. "We call Molly Crane."

The barmaid, maintaining self-assured importance, strolled to the witness stand.

"Molly Crane, do you swear and affirm that the testimony you are about to give is the truth, so help you, God?" asked the magistrate.

"I do affirm, Your Lordship."

"Molly Crane, do you know these men?" the magistrate asked.

"Aye, Your Lordship. They came into the Green Hog. By their manner of speech and queries, I imagined they escaped from a lunatic asylum."

A flurry of laughter erupted.

"What kind of queries?" asked the barrister.

"They sez they are from a village called Milwaukee. They asked me where they were. I sez, 'England' and thinking they a playing some type of joke on me."

"They asked you where they were?" the barrister inquired, showing visible surprise.

"Aye, and they even asked me what year it was."

The assembly exploded into laughter.

"Is that all?"

"No, Your Lordship. They paid for their meal and drink with strange money."

"Strange money?"

"Aye. It said, 'The United States of America.'"

"What was so strange about that?"

"I believed me eyes deceived me, your Lordship when I sees a coin as 1998."

The gathering let out a collective gasp.

"Do you have that money on your person?" asked the barrister.

"Aye," Molly said before reaching into a fold of her dress to extract the coins.

She held them out to the barrister, who cupped the coins in his hand and examined them.

A collective curiosity arose among the attendees, many of whom stretched their necks in the direction of the barrister.

He handed them up to the magistrate.

"Molly Crane, do you have any more to say about these men?" the magistrate asked, pointing to the accused.

"Aye, Your Lordship."

Adam and Kyle squirmed within their enclosed perch.

"When they sat down at me table, they asked for a 'burger.'"

"A burger?"

"Aye, Your Lordship."

Again, more laughter radiated among those present.

The magistrate shouted over the hilarity, "Molly Crane, you may step down."

Returning to her seat, she held her head high, her contempt for the accused evident as she passed Adam and Kyle.

The justice of the peace and magistrate drew closer, their backs to the assembly, and began their deliberations. Moments later, they resumed their positions and faced the assembly.

The justice of the peace resumed his post. "Adam Cabano, and Kyle Kroft, having been charged with the crime of murder, this court finds a true bill against you as evidence of your guilt. Therefore, the court doth order you to be taken from hence to Newcastle, where you shall appear before a grand jury for your crime. Do you have anything to say in your defense?"

"We didn't do it," Kyle bawled.

"We're innocent. We found that gun on the road," Adam shouted, his manacled hands waving wildly and noisily in the air.

"The bailiff will remove the accused and confine them until transportation can be arranged. And may the Lord have mercy upon your souls."

CHAPTER NINETEEN

"The Repo Man"

Detective Morris parked his blue Subaru Forester a block away from the Acme Movers and Storage Company. Set in Milwaukee's industrial Menomonee Valley area, the business was a low-key operation that paled in appearance next to its more vibrant-looking neighbors.

Officer Dunlap immediately grabbed the binoculars for a closer view. "It seems that only Tony's driver is getting out."

"That can only mean one thing—Tony's making another stop," said Morris, who was about to turn off the engine but drew his hand away from the ignition button.

"Hey, he's coming out already," exclaimed Dunlap.

One of the rollup doors opened, and a small van displaying the company's logo pulled out onto the street. Tony's black Mercedes moved ahead. As it eased forward, the truck followed.

Shadowing the mini-convoy, Morris kept a safe distance as they wound their way through the industrial park. Turning south onto 16th

Street, he slipped the Forester into the flowing traffic and followed at a closer distance.

"They're turning east onto Lapham," said Morris as he switched lanes. "It's no coincidence they chose that street. My guess, whatever they are up to involves Adam Cabano and Kyle Kroft's place."

"Do you have any clue or hunch what this is all about?"

"Shit, the light's changing," said Morris as he abruptly came to a stop behind two other vehicles. He hit the steering wheel with the palm of his hand. "I haven't a clue what this is all about."

"Maybe this will be a big break in the case?"

"I don't know. None of this stuff is making any sense. And from what I've seen so far, none of the dots are connecting."

"If we could only get hold of Adam and Kyle, we'd at least have some idea what's going on."

"That's a big if, and from my experience, these lowlife crooks tend to clam up under questioning," said Morris, who was nervously drumming his fingers on the center console.

"Green arrow," hollered Dunlap.

Turning onto Lapham, Morris stomped on the accelerator and weaved his way around the slower-moving cars.

"It's good you're a cop, or I'd have to give you a ticket."

"Well, I'm trying to make up for the lost time, in case I'm wrong about their destination."

"As long as we arrive in one piece," retorted Dunlap, who grabbed the overhead handle to steady herself.

Morris eased up on the gas pedal. "It looks like it's our lucky day." He parked a block short of the Acme truck and shut off his engine.

Once again, Dunlap used the binoculars to gain a better view. "I don't see Tony's car. Wait, now I see him—he's parked down the street. The engine is running, and both men are in the car."

Morris held out his hand. "Let me have a gander."

Dunlap leaned back in her seat and crossed her arms over her chest. "Hey, my eyes are as good as yours ... maybe better," she said offishly.

He turned toward her. "Yeah, yeah, I'm sure they are. I only wanted to see for myself. Didn't they give you sensitivity training in the academy?" Looking back down the street, he said, "That's interesting."

"What?" she asked, arms still crossed.

"That guy I talked with last time we were here, he's leading those *Acme* workers back to Kyle and Adam's place. And that Ford truck of theirs is gone."

"How do you know that? You can't even see beyond the first couple of feet of the driveway from this angle."

He handed the binoculars back to Dunlap. "Last time, the landlord's Caddy was crowding the front walkway. Now I don't see it. It must be in his garage."

"Do you think they skipped town?"

"I don't know. I'm interested in what those two goons want from our boys."

Dunlap took the eyeglasses and resumed her watch. Within only a few minutes of their departure, the Acme employees reappeared carrying an ornate chair.

"What the hell?" she cried and handed the glasses back to Detective Morris.

"Wow. This case just got curiouser and curiouser," he said.

"Could it be an antique chair that's got Tony in such a state?"

Morris shook his head. "I'm no antique dealer. It's hard to tell from this distance."

"Maybe there's jewels and stuff like that shoved into the cushions?"

"I doubt it. If it were something like that, Tony would have his minions handle it. He a good administrator—that's what makes this whole caper so unusual. They're going to take that chair somewhere, and when they do, we'll be following them."

"By the looks of it, they're handling it with kid gloves. So, it must be valuable."

"So, Rick, it looks like I may be right. I mean about the antique angle."

A smile gradually formed on Morris's face. "Rick?"

"Yeah, it's better than some of the other names I thought of using."

"Okay, Susan, in this car, we're on a first-name basis."

"Gotcha, Rick," she said hesitantly. "And it appears our pickup van is about to leave."

Morris turned on the ignition but left the car in park. "I don't want to spook 'em." He checked his rearview mirror. "There's a couple of cars heading this way. I'll pull in behind them to give us more cover." As they passed, he put his Subaru in gear and eased out into the street.

The traffic was moderate until they approached the vicinity of Jones Island. Easing back in the thin traffic flow, they trailed near enough to keep an eye on the vehicles without arousing any suspicion. When Tony's Mercedes led the van into a storage facility, Rick continued past the entrance, knowing it was the end of the line.

CHAPTER TWENTY

"A Good Day for a Hanging"

Roused from their sleep, Adam and Kyle were herded through the darkness toward a prison van by two guards. Unlike their earlier keepers, they wore uniforms. Each man had a narrow-brimmed, tall cylindrical top hat.

"Step lively, lads," the taller guard with mutton chops urged. 'Yer'in only an 'alf-day's journey from a meeting your maker in Newcastle."

Sluggishly placing his foot into the wagon's rear step, Adam gradually pressed his way beneath the low interior and crawled forward.

Kyle resisted and fought his handlers, his chains rattling as he tried to pull away. In the scuffle, the taller guard poked him with a truncheon.

"Come on, lad. You be missin' Throttler Smith if ye don't hurry," said the shorter of the two men who held a lantern high in the air.

Both guards laughed heartily.

As Kyle mounted the van, he glanced back and asked, "Who's Throttler Smith?"

"Why, he be yer hangman, by jiminy."

Again, the guards let out a riotous laugh. They slammed the door on the prison van. After securing the padlock, they moved forward and took their place in the driver's box—the faint glow of the lantern following them.

Three barred openings admitted a small amount of moonlight, which was further lessened by the thin layer of overcast skies. Their advancement over the unlit rutted roads, and the periodic unveiling of the full-moon, did little to improve their ability to see.

Kyle, sitting with a knotted posture across from Adam and studying the floor, glanced up. "You ain't said nothing since we got on this shit wagon. Aren't you scared?"

"I've been thinking."

"Yeah, I've been thinking, too. Like how's it's gonna feel having my neck stretched."

"No, numbnuts. I've been thinking about how we're going to escape."

"You got a plan?"

"Yeah, I got a plan. And I think it'll work. Here it is, so listen up. When we get to this place, they're taking us—we jump the guards. We take the keys, then get back to that dude ranch, or whatever it is."

"How we gonna do that?" asked Kyle.

"We've got surprise on our side."

"Surprise?"

"Yeah. We get close to the door when we stop. After the screws unlock it, we jump out and attack them."

"And yell surprise?"

"Yeah, what the hell—you can holler surprise if you want. The whole idea is to take them off guard. I'm banking on them not expecting us to do that."

"What if they shoot us?"

"They ain't got a hand cannon, so we're safe."

Kyle nodded.

The lingering silence that followed Adam's unveiling of his plan finally ended when he spoke up. "Ya, know, I didn't kill that guy."

"Huh? I saw you. You snuffed him," Kyle said.

"How old are you?"

"Twenty-three."

"When's your birthday."

"What has—"

"Just tell me your birthday, shithead," ordered Adam.

"July 25, 1996."

"Okay. When did that guy die?"

"That lady in the restaurant said it was eighteen ..." Kyle faltered.

"Eighteen fifty-four. Now, subtract the year 1854 from 1996."

"Ah ..."

"Careful, you'll blow a fuse on that brain of yours—that's 142 years before you were born."

Kyle looked at Adam in puzzlement. "I don't get it."

"It's simple. In 1996, the year you were born, that guy was already dead. So, I didn't kill him. He was already dead."

Judging from his reaction, Adam knew he didn't understand. "Don't worry about it. According to that tall guard, we got a way to go. So, try to get some rest."

———

The uneven gait of the horses, the smell of smoke, and a slight tremor awakened Adam. Pulling himself to the window, he craned his neck to eye an enormous fire that engulfed several buildings. "Get up and take a look at this," he yelled.

Kyle crowded Adam for a glimpse. "Wow, that's one big-ass fire."

There was an animated exchange between the guards from on top of the driver's box, their voices rising as the wagon edged forward. The pace quickened, and it was apparent to Adam that the driver wanted to put distance between himself and the fire. As they continued to move, they observed the silhouettes of the curious, backlighted by the fire, lining the railings of the bridge. Adam and Kyle scrambled to the rear of the wagon, trying for a better view. The inferno's heat reached into the wagon's interior as they began traveling to the other side of the river.

While captivated by the enormity of the blaze, they were momentarily blinded by an explosion. A thunderous shockwave from the blast struck the wagon with the intensity of an earthquake. The horses screamed as the wagon began to roll over while at the same time being pounded with a hail of bricks. Kyle and Adam, futilely reaching for anything to stabilize themselves, tumbled from floor to wall as the wagon crashed onto its side. With a jarring thud and stunned, they fell onto the wall of the wagon as the door split in two. Bruised and disorientated, they began to crawl their way to freedom.

All about them, bodies littered the roadway. Screams of the injured filled the air while the long shadows of the fleeing danced on the road. People cried out in pain while others remained still, the severity of their wounds indicating their fate. Adam and Kyle moved their way forward. The guards, too, lay near the dead horses, one of the men crushed under the horse's bulk.

"We ain't got but this one chance," Adam said as he reached for the keys fastened to the belt of the taller man.

Semiconscious, the guard, bleeding from his head and sprawled among the wreckage, made a feeble attempt to block Adam by drawing his truncheon.

With harsh cruelty, Adam stomped on the guard's arm, forcing the man to relinquish the club. Yanking the keys from him, he freed himself and Kyle before pitching them into the river below.

Shrouded within the chaos and free of their chains, Adam and Kyle blended into the melee of fleeing evacuees.

CHAPTER TWENTY-ONE

"Eye in the Sky"

Tony, his arms crossed, stood admiring the six monitors on the back wall of the custodian's shack.

Chuck, indifferent to the new security addition, waited uneasily for Tony's next command.

"Chuck, this is a state-of-the-art security system. Everything will be recorded, including your regular night rounds. You got that?"

"Yes, Mr. Angelo," he answered, nervously shifting in place.

"If your mother weren't my mother's friend, you'd be without a job and living under the Hoan Bridge. Lucky for you, I got my stuff back. So, you better not let anything happen to my storage locker again. *Capisce?*"

"Yes, Mr. Angelo."

Tony pointed to the top center screen, which displayed a static image of his personal locker. "Pay close attention to that one."

"I will, Mr. Angelo."

"Good. I already went through this with my cousin Richie. The system runs itself. It even has a battery backup. All you have to do is pay attention."

Chuck nodded.

"Oh, and by the way. Richie's sister, Martha, is getting married this Saturday. I'll have one of my men filling in for him on his dayshift."

Chuck nodded again.

"I got to get going. I have to take care of some stuff, but I'll be back later this evening."

Tony let himself out and got into his waiting Mercedes.

CHAPTER TWENTY-TWO

"Wazup?"

While standing at his office window, Captain Ed Chalmers gazed down on the early morning traffic below. "What happened after Tony left his storage facility?" he asked Detective Morris without turning around.

Morris, sitting in the chair next to Officer Dunlap, leaned back. "He went straight to his home in Waukesha. We watched his place until Tony's driver parked the Mercedes in the garage. I figured he was in for the rest of the night."

Chalmers turned and returned to his desk, then sat down. "So, you're telling me this whole thing is over a lousy chair?"

Morris shrugged. "Yeah, I guess so."

"What about those two clowns, Adam Cabano and Kyle ... what's his name?" asked Chalmers.

"Kroft," interrupted Officer Dunlap.

"Yeah, what about them?"

"After tailing Tony back to his place, Officer Dunlap and I went to their house on Lapham. I didn't want to ask the landlord and blow my cover, so Dunlap went there instead."

Chalmers looked at Dunlap. "What did you learn from him?"

She cleared her throat. "He told me he hadn't seen either of them in almost a week, and their rent is past due. The landlord also said some furniture company repossessed their chair."

"Yeah, I was curious how Tony's people were able to walk in and take it without any fuss," Morris said.

"You don't think Tony had those two guys bumped off, do you?"

"I don't think so, Captain," answered Morris. "If that were the case, he wouldn't be asking around trying to find them. No, I think they just flew the coop."

"Ya know, we're not going to be able to drill down to the bedrock of this story unless we find those two guys," Captain Chalmers said. "They have to have some girlfriends, brothers or sisters. Check with missing persons and see if anyone reported them as AWOL."

Morris got up. "Will do, Captain," he said and moved near the door. With Dunlap close behind, he paused and turned toward Chalmers. "I did some research on Tony's storage facility. He bought it for a song back in 1974 because the economy was in the crapper at the time. I understand he's been offered big bucks for it from a few cartage companies, but he won't budge. Maybe it's sentimental?"

"It's more than that," replied Chalmers. "When I was a rookie cop, the area around Jones Island was part of my beat. There were a lot more scrap metal operations and other crappy establishments at the time. At night, we'd run into some pretty unsavory characters. Anyway, that's another story. What I was getting at was as soon as Tony started that storage business, his empire grew. The bunko division started to pay closer attention to him, as well as the Feds."

Morris removed his hand from the doorknob. "Did they raid the place?"

"Yeah, several times, and each time it came up clean."

"So, Captain, are you saying that we'll be wasting our time?"

"No, I'm not saying that at all. What I want you to do is pay close attention to this case because I think it may be the linchpin to the entire operation."

———

There was an approaching sound of shuffling feet as Detective Morris and Officer Dunlap waited outside the apartment of Katharine Kroft. Her name, etched in the door's brass nameplate with Victorian fonts, yawned open and transported them into the fantasy world of Jules Verne. Standing between them and a mystifying collection of eclectic steampunk possessions stood a tall, beautiful young girl with brassy orange hair and a labret piercing below her lip.

Morris guessed her to be in her mid-twenties. "Miss Kroft, I am Detective Morris, and this is Officer Dunlap." He flashed his badge. Dunlap did the same. "You reported that your brother Kyle was missing."

"Yes, I did. I'm surprised you're here so quickly because I reported it only this morning."

"We'd like to get some more information from you. May we come in?" asked Morris.

"Sure." She directed them toward a leather couch arrayed with a series of bronze studs decorating its framework.

"You have quite an unusual place," remarked Officer Dunlap as she sat down onto the plush cushion.

"I assume that was a compliment?"

"It was," she answered, her attention quickly diverted to the rest of the apartment.

Morris cleared his throat. "About your missing brother."

"Yes. Kyle calls me at least every couple of days, usually asking me for money or some other favor. After four days, I decided to file a report with the Milwaukee Police Department."

"Do you know anything about Adam Cabano?" asked Morris.

She eased back into her large Queen Ann leather armchair, flipping her brown ruffled skirt over her crossed legs. Immediately her demeanor changed. "Yeah, I know him. He's a bad influence on Kyle. You're not here to tell me that my brother's dead, are you?"

Morris waved a dismissive hand. "No, no, nothing like that. We only know that your brother hangs out with him."

Katharine Kroft leaned forward and rested an elbow on her knee.

"A while ago, Kyle brought that Adam creep with him. After they left, I discovered some money was missing from my kitchen counter. I told Kyle never to bring him here again." She resumed her laid-back position.

"Besides Adam Cabano, does Kyle have any other friends, or say a girlfriend?" asked Morris, his notebook at the ready.

She shook her head. "No to having a girlfriend. He can barely support himself. I'm sorry, detective, I know very little about the things he does, other than the fact that he doesn't have a girlfriend. I do know he plays pool. And from what I can tell, that's how he earns his money."

"So, he doesn't have a job?"

"No, detective. He once worked for a janitorial service, but that was a few years ago. Quite frankly, and you probably may suspect this, too, I'm guessing he's into some pretty unsavory stuff as long as he continues to hang with that bum, Adam."

"Ah, Miss Kroft," Officer Dunlap began, her eyes giving the room the once over. "You have a lovely and unique apartment. What exactly do you do for a living?"

"I can assure you—it's legal, and people pay me well for my handiwork."

"Dunlap turned a shade of pink. "Oh, I didn't mean anything by that, Miss Kroft. I really like the place. I'm just curious."

Kroft forced a smile. "Thank you. I am an interior decorator and metal sculptress." She pointed toward a sculpture of a nude woman constructed from consecutive layers of metal. "That's one of my most recent creations."

"Wow, that is impressive," exclaimed Dunlap.

Morris cleared his throat then rose from the couch. Dunlap followed his lead. He handed Kroft his card. "Feel free to contact us if your brother should show up before we locate him."

"I will, detective. And could you do me a favor?"

"What's that?" asked Morris.

"Lock up, Adam. I'm sure you'll find some excuse for putting him in jail."

Morris only nodded.

CHAPTER TWENTY-THREE

"Tallyho!"

Weaving their way through the sea of confusion, Adam and Kyle sought refuge in the periphery of the mayhem. Studying the commotion from the blown-in remains of a clothing store, they watched as columns of smoke twisted upward while leaping flames devoured more buildings.

"I've never seen anything like this in my life," Kyle said.

"Yeah, me, too," Adam agreed.

"What do we do now?"

Adam retreated farther into the structure. "We gotta get back to that mansion and out of this bizarro time."

"How we gonna do that?"

"We can't go back to that town because someone will recognize us. We gotta find another way." Aided by the glow from the fires, Adam inspected the interior of the shop. "We need to ditch our threads, or at least put something over them."

Kyle moved to the shop's back, where most of the clothing lay

bunched into several heaps and covered with lath and plaster fragments. As he rummaged through the clutter, he found a long frock
coat. He slipped it over his fatigue jacket. "It's a little tight."

"It's okay. Yah ain't modeling for *Rolling Stone*."

Following several attempts, Adam uncovered a tan duster that
adequately concealed his peacoat. He shoved his baseball cap into one
of the pockets. Topping off his new look, he retrieved a grey slouch
hat, while Kyle located a black Victorian top hat. Before leaving, each
man grabbed a printed red paisley handkerchief to serve as a bandana
against the intensifying clouds of smoke.

The two of them, both dressed in their new yet soiled apparel,
began to mingle with the confused masses. Putting distance between
the crowds and any connection to the overturned prison wagon, they
hurriedly fled the area.

The pair wove in and out of the flame-licked shadows as they
retreated to the outskirts of Gateshead. Worn out and dog-tired, they
found a grassy knoll on which to crash. Along with a few trees, the tall
grass gave them adequate cover. From their position, Adam and Kyle
watched as the horizon glowed with spiraling columns of smoke that
twisted ceaselessly into the morning sky. Amide the inferno, people,
illuminated by its glow, ebbed and flowed from view, never seeming to
have a purpose.

"I've never seen a fire that humongous," Kyle said.

Adam nodded. "Yeah, that's one helluva fire."

"What do we do now?"

"Nothing," Adam answered sharply. "First, I gotta get some sleep,
then I'll think of something." He looked around and saw only a few
distant cottages. Thinking the area safe, he lay down in the tall grass
and curled into a fetal position. After placing his slouch hat over his
face to block the gaining daylight, he closed his eyes.

Fashioning a pillow out of his fatigue jacket, Kyle covered himself
with the long coat and fell fast asleep.

———

Awakened by the sound of a distant train's whistle, Adam rose and stretched in place. He kicked the bottom of Kyle's boots. "Time to get going," he said, looking north at the smoldering ruins of the towns.

Kyle peered out of his makeshift cover. "I'm starving," he said, squinting at the noontime sun. He slowly got to his feet and joined Adam as he watched both towns, on either side of the river, continue to burn.

"Yeah, we gotta get something to eat."

"A restaurant?"

Adam shook his head. "You remember what happened the last time we ate in a restaurant. No, we gotta steal our grub this time."

"Which way do we go?"

"I ain't got a clue, only that we need to go somewhere south, toward the sun. We'll have to ask someone for directions."

"That hottress said the town was called Bolden, New something or other," Kyle said, still captivated by the burning towns.

"Winning, I think. C'mon, we gotta get going," Adam said as he proceeded down the backside of the hill.

Upon reaching a road, they met a rider making his way in the fire's direction.

"Good, sirs," the man called out, pulling up on the reins. "I beg your pardon. I infer by your travel that you have seen the fire?"

"Ahh ... yeah," Adam said.

"Yankee men, are you?"

Remembering the waitress's words about sailors, Adam nodded. "Yeah, our ship burned in the fire."

"I say, poor fellow, what a misfortune. Are you gentlemen lost?"

Kyle was about to say something before Adam intervened. "We are. We're on the way to Boldin New Winnings."

"Gentlemen, you are off your course. Boldon New Winning is due east." The man pointed. "I should think you will be able to be there in three hours."

"Thanks. We lost all of our things when our ship sunk. We have a friend in New Winnings."

"My name is Dr. Samuel Nicholas, sir," the man said while removing his hat.

"I'm Adam, and this is Kyle. We are without money and hungry. Like I said, we lost everything in the fire. We hope to get some help from our friend."

"Gentlemen, I have the satisfaction to have made your acquaintance. Allow me, sirs, to pay for your fare at the Golden Galleon, a pub only a half-mile from here." He reached into his coat pocket then bent down to hand Adam a few coins. "That should help feed your stomachs and provide you with enough sustenance until you reach your destination. Remain on this road until you reach the bottom of the hill."

"Thanks, mister," Adam said, nodding his gratefulness.

"Upon my word," exclaimed Nicholas, "it is a most fortunate, indeed, that our paths should have crossed. Now, good fortune and good day to you, both. After hearing of your misadventure, I'm most certain my services are needed in Gateshead."

He replaced his hat, tipped it in parting, and galloped off.

CHAPTER TWENTY-FOUR

"Door Number One, or Door Number Two?"

Officer Dunlap sat on the edge of the passenger side seat of the Subaru. Leaning forward, she steadied her hold on the binoculars by placing her elbows on the car's dashboard. She pulled away and eased back into the seat. "It's been two days, and we haven't seen anyone, other than the watchmen, coming or going from Tony's storage place. How long do you think we'll have to be here, I mean, on this case?"

Detective Morris yawned and scratched the back of his neck. "I don't know. Sometimes it can take months of surveillance work. I'll tell you one thing about this case I don't like."

"What's that?"

"We don't have a clear view of all those storage lockers. And we can't get any closer than a block without arousing suspicion."

"Why can't we stake out the place from that old warehouse?" she pointed toward a white four-storied building near the backside of the storage facility. "It looks abandoned."

"Nothing is truly abandoned in Milwaukee. Someone or some

company always owns the property. If the Milwaukee Police Department were to ask permission to use the building for a stakeout, the owner would want some rent money. And besides, maybe the owner knows Tony, and the owner blows our cover."

"Okay, let's say we, as police officers, happened to be traveling past. Let's say—we hear a noise from inside that building. What do you think we should do?"

"Ah, what exactly did you do when you were in the army?" Morris asked, giving her a look of surprise.

"Intelligence."

"Okay. Say we follow your plan. How do we get in?"

"When I was in Afghanistan, and we needed to get into a building, we simply broke in."

"Who are you? Batwoman?"

"Ha, ha. So, Dudley Do-Right, whaddya think?"

"Your plan has some merit," Morris said as he started the car's engine. "I'm not gonna commit to it, but let's take a ride."

Approaching the building, Morris parked his Subaru on the opposite side of the street. The building appeared to have been a factory, or perhaps the corpse of a company forced into extinction by a foreign corporation. The soiled "For-Sale" sign begged for a new owner. The neighborhood itself was a mix of neglected residences owned by absentee landlords and warehouses that appeared unused. Some of the homes revealed the telltale evidence of habitation with people engaged in television amusements.

"C'mon," he urged as he slid out of his seat.

After dismissing the idea of going through the padlocked front door, they moved down the street to a dead-end alleyway.

"This is the backside of Tony's storage place. It doesn't look promising," Morris said. "Besides, if we get any closer, we'll be in the range of that." He pointed toward a security camera mounted above a triple row of barbed wire, laced over a chain-linked section of fencing.

"What about the other side?" asked Dunlap. "There was a flimsy-looking fence between this building and the neighboring one."

"Yeah, I saw it, too. I came here first because I thought it would be less conspicuous."

Turning away and moving down the dead-end alleyway, Morris halted abruptly and pushed back Dunlap. "This old factory now has some activity."

She gave him a puzzled look. "What do you mean?"

"You didn't see what I saw a second ago. A couple of shady-looking types just went in the front door. Considering the hour, I'm guessing they're up to no good."

"If they went in the front door, that means they have a key. Maybe they own the building?"

"They didn't look like the landlord type. One thing, it provides us an excuse to get inside and have a look-see. Let's give 'em some time until the hook's set," Morris said before leading Dunlap back into the shadows.

"How much time do you think we need?"

"Just a couple of minutes. I'm guessing they're gonna head down to the basement or the top floors."

Morris moved to the dumpster and lifted its cover. Looking inside, he quickly drew back and closed the lid. "They'll be on the top floor."

"What makes you say that?"

"If they were using the place for storage of fenced goods, the basement. In this case, it's a meth lab. They need ventilation. The top floor is their best choice."

Dunlap peered into the dumpster. "Ewww, that's disgusting. It smells like urine."

"Yeah, I'm sure they figured that no one would be the wiser by getting rid of their junk in that. The trash service never looks in the dumpster when they pick up."

"Aren't you going to call for backup?"

"Remember, we're here to keep tabs on Tony's storage place. Hopefully, it will be a quiet bust. The door had a chain lock around its handle, and I saw only two men enter—tells me we can handle it. After we nab these guys, we'll call it in."

"Are you sure? I mean, it could get dicey," said Dunlap as she drew her gun to check its clip.

"A Sig?" asked Morris.

"Yeah, a P226. I had one in Afghanistan. I liked it so much that, when I came back to the States, I bought one for myself."

"And the department okayed it?" he asked in surprise.

"Yeah, considering my familiarity with it and experience, it was allowed."

"I hope we won't need it. C'mon, let's see what's going on."

Morris slid an expired Barnes and Noble membership card between the lock and doorjamb.

"That's a pretty neat trick. I take it you've done this before," whispered Dunlap.

"A few," he said before drawing his Glock while entering the building.

Guided by the faint light from a nearby streetlamp that spilled in through side windows along the stairwell, they slowly inched their way upward. Months, perhaps years of debris, littered their path, making each step at risk to detection. As they reached the top floor, a blueish glow radiated from a slightly ajar door. The pungent smell of acetone drifted into the vestibule.

Morris, his weapon at the ready, went to the open side. Dunlap moved across from him. He nodded.

With both hands gripping his Glock, he kicked the door open and yelled, "Police! Freeze!"

Dunlap, aiming her Sig forward, moved into the breach, then crouched down.

Two men, their faces covered with respirators, stiffened.

"You're under arrest. Your hands, get 'em up," Morris ordered.

The men raised their latex-gloved hands.

"Get away from the table," he commanded, coaxing them with a wave of his handgun. "C'mon, move it!"

Both men, dressed in jeans and flannel shirts, unhurriedly moved to the side.

"Okay, that's far enough. Now, slowly, remove your masks," said Morris.

Each man grasped the straps with two hands and pulled off the gas masks, dropping them to their side.

One of the men appeared to be Hispanic and in his late-twenties. The other man, black, maybe younger, shuffled uneasily in place.

The Latino's eyes shifted.

Morris, detecting the movement in the man's eyes, turned slightly to spot two more men. Each man started to go for their weapons. Whirling to the side, he fired four shots before either of them could bring their guns to play.

Dunlap was temporarily distracted during the shooting. She looked back at the meth lab felons as the black man began to lower his arms. "Don't even think of it," she commanded. "Turn around and get down. Now!"

Morris rushed over to the fallen men and kicked away their weapons. Leaning down, he checked the first man's pulse. "This one's gone."

Turning to the next one, he yelled, "Call 911! This one's bailing."

While making the call, Dunlap, using her foot, forced the men to spread their legs. "Now cup your hands behind your heads. Hurry up."

The piercing howl of a siren grew louder.

CHAPTER TWENTY-FIVE

"You Don't Say?"

The Golden Galleon tavern appeared deserted. Adam cautiously tried the door and found it unlocked. Like the Green Hog, it, too, was rustic yet lacked customers or the welcoming warmth of a fire. Only a solitary lantern lighted the interior.

From a partially hidden nook, a burly-looking man emerged.

"I'm very sorry, gentlemen, but I'm on my own. My help left for Gateshead, and I haven't had time to set the fire."

"Do you have anything to eat?" Adam asked, rubbing his hands.

"Yankee men, are you?" the pub owner remarked.

"Yeah, sailors." They drew closer to the man.

"My name is James Bond." Motioning with his thumb, Adam said, "And this is my friend Clint Eastwood."

"I'm Henry Ludlow, the proprietor of this pub." He rested his arms on the counter that separated them. He appeared to study his new patrons with hesitation. His gaze fell on Adam's shoes. "That's a most unusual shoe."

"Yeah, they're called sneakers."

"I don't recall seeing anything like them before."

"They're new in the States," snapped Adam. "Hey, mister. We are starving and would like something to eat."

The man withdrew his muscular arms from the counter. "I should think you would have found food in Gateshead with the rest of your crew."

"They all died in the fire. The ship sunk, and we are lucky to be alive," said Adam. "The whole town is on fire."

The owner's eyes bulged in apparent surprise. "Your news is most distressing. We heard the explosion and most of our people went to see what happened. I'd have gone myself but was not up to dick, feeling as poorly as I am. What was the name of your ship?"

"Ah ... the Black Pearl."

"The name is not familiar. What's your captain's name? We do have an occasional visit from Yankee men."

"Ah ... Captain Jack Sparrow. He died when the ship sunk. Please, mister. Do you have any food?" begged Adam.

"Aye. Without my cook, all I have to offer is some bread and pickled eggs."

Adam reached into his pocket. Placing the coins onto the counter, he said, "We met a Dr. Nicholas on our way here. He gave us this money for a meal."

The proprietor slid the change back to Adam. "The doctor is an upright man. You can keep your coppers. Mr. Bond and Mr. Eastwood, I would be most thankful for a firsthand account of your ship and how it came to be lost. Put your hats here on the counter, then step over near the hearth. I will set us a fire."

Once Adam and Kyle seated themselves at the table, the owner bent down and struck a match to light a clump of kindling. Using a metal poker to push small logs onto the fire, he nurtured it into a roaring blaze. Leaving the two, he quickly returned with a platter of bread and a jar of pickled eggs.

"Here, gentlemen, spoon out your eggs while I go fetch some beer."

Although alone, Kyle leaned over, and in a secretive manner, asked, "What'll you tell him?" He scooped out a brownish egg from the jar.

Adam grabbed a piece of bread. "I'll tell him how we escaped."

"How will you bullshit him? You've never been on a ship."

"Leave it to me. Keep your yap shut. Just nod and fill your pie hole."

Kyle scrunched his face. "This egg tastes funny."

"Ain't you ever had pickled eggs before?"

"Yeah, but they were white."

Adam reached for the spoon and scooped out an egg. He took a bite. "I see what you mean, but it ain't all that bad." He popped the rest of it into his mouth then chomped down on his slice of bread. "There, that's how you do it," he muttered, his cheeks bulging.

The owner returned with a pitcher of beer in one hand and three glass mugs in the other. "Gentlemen, I'm sorry for the meager meal, but enliven yourselves with me beer."

Filling the mugs, Henry Ludlow then sat down on the other side of the table. His gaze jumped from man to man as he appeared to study them more closely. "Please, having been in Gateshead at the time of the explosion, I'm most eager to hear your account and escape."

Adam took a big swallow, cupped his hand over his mouth, then wiped off the excess beer. He cleared his throat. "We were sleeping in our beds and woke up when we heard this huge explosion. The ship rolled over, and we fell onto the floor."

"Ah, if your ship was on its side, you mean bulkhead, don't you?" asked Ludlow.

"Yeah, yeah, sure. We fell on the, ah ... bulkhead. Well, it happened so sudden like, that we didn't know what happened. Me and my pal, Eastwood here, ran upstairs."

"If the ship was on its side, how did you get topside?"

"Ya see, we were near the door leading to the up ... I mean, topside. So, all we had to do was crawl out of the doorway. Then the ship started to sink."

"What about the rest of the crew? Didn't they come out with you?"

"They were in a different room and were trapped when the ship sunk."

Ludlow took a sip of beer. He put down his mug, crossed his arms, and leaned back in his chair. "That is a very fascinating account, Mr.

Bond. What about your officers? You must have had an executive officer. What happened to him?"

"Ah ... that was Commander Spock."

"And what happened to him?" Ludlow asked again, his body stiffening.

"He was trapped, too. And then the ship caught fire. So, Kyle ... ah, Mr. Eastwood and I jumped onto the dock and ran away."

Ludlow eyed Kyle, who nodded in agreement. "You said the whole town started to burn. Most ships dock on the quayside of Newcastle along The River Tyne. How did you get on the other side to Gateshead? I should have thought you would have found the hills, north of the river, a more desirable escape route."

Kyle shifted in place.

Adam's mouth became dry. He grabbed his beer then took a hurried swallow. "Ah ... the hills were on fire. We just ran across the bridge." Feeling the heat from the fireplace and the increased questioning, he reached inside his coat pocket for the red kerchief. He wiped his brow, unaware that his Milwaukee Brewer's cap had also fallen out.

Ludlow glanced at the floor and then back at Adam before jumping to his feet. He snatched the poker from the fireplace and held it out like a sword. "Don't sell me a dog. Your story's a flam, and I heard all about your murderous deed. You think I'm a little nickey in the head, trying to spin your yarn. You're no sailors. You're due for a topping, and I'll lead you to the gallows myself." He moved menacingly toward Adam.

Kyle rose, lunged at Ludlow but was thwarted by Ludlow's metal poker as he jammed it into Kyle's stomach. Shrieking in pain, he doubled over and fell to the floor.

As Adam sped to Kyle's defense, his chair made a sharp barking sound as it skidded over the stone floor. Using what was available, he used his mug as a hammer and struck the pub owner's forehead.

Dazed, Ludlow staggered backward, his nose bleeding. The owner, now appearing disorientated from the blow, struggled to regain balance before striking his head on the fireplace's mantel. Falling into a heap of disheveled blood-soaked clothing, he lay motionless at the base of the hearth.

CHAPTER TWENTY-SIX

"The After-action Report"

Captain Ed Chalmers finished closing the blinds on his office windows before sitting down at his desk.

"You know the drill," he began, focusing his attention on Detective Morris. "I had to turn over your gun to ballistics. Since Officer Dunlap didn't fire her weapon, she will be the only one carrying until the *shooting team* finishes their investigation. Your story that you were casing the warehouse for illegal activity provides some cover for the real reason you were there. Great job to both of you."

"Thanks, Captain," Morris said.

"By the way, you two were damn lucky not to be blown to smithereens. Firing your gun in a meth lab could have been disastrous."

"The toxic fumes?" asked Dunlap.

"Yeah, sometimes they go *kaboom*," Chalmers said. "Now, let's get down to business."

"And the bust?" Morris asked.

"We'll just let the investigation run its course. But, here's the thing.

Officially, you're on administrative leave. But I'm not going to object if you help Officer Dunlap."

Morris frowned. "What do you mean? You know the routine, all those involved in a shooting go on administrative leave."

"I was able to pull some big strings to keep her on the case. At this point, we cannot take a chance by not having anyone cover that locker between four and midnight. Officer Dunlap, do you mind taking over the operation until Detective Morris resumes his regular assignment?"

"No, Captain," she said, her face beaming.

"Great. Now, Morris, did you have the toxicology test and schedule an appointment with the department's psychiatrist?"

"Yep," he said curtly.

"Good. Now I want to go over the plan I devised for using the warehouse as a base of operations."

———

Dunlap flashed her badge at one of the policemen on duty as she entered the warehouse, with Morris in tow.

"He's with me," she said and shot a thumb in Morris's direction, slipping past the security detail. "We're going to be here for a couple of hours."

"Well, I won't," said one of the cops. "Our relief is coming in about an hour. Where are you two going? The top floor is off-limits."

"Don't worry, we'll only be on the second floor," she called back, taking a few steps onto the stairwell.

"We'll let our relief know you're here."

"Thanks," Morris said, bringing up the rear. He pointed at the lighted exit sign. "It appears the electricity is back on."

Dunlap pulled open the second story's fire door. The exit sign over the door barely gave them enough light by which to see. "It looks like admin stuff on this floor—or perhaps billing and shipping."

The two of them gradually felt their way through a maze of partitions and dim security lighting before finding a window that overlooked Tony Angelo's storage facility.

Now bathed in the light from the outside security lighting, Morris cranked open a window. The late afternoon's chill and harbor's pong spilled into the area. Along with the intense smell from the port, the distant clang of a buoy wafted in. With a hushed voice, he asked, "Okay, now the boring stuff begins. What's your plan, boss?"

"Hey, Rick. You know that Captain Chalmers said I was in charge only because of the shooting?"

"Yeah, I know. I was only messing with you."

"So, what do we do?"

"We sit and trade-off napping until midnight, waiting for something to happen. But considering this place isn't heated, I don't think you'll have trouble keeping awake."

Dunlap popped up on a desk, stretched out her legs, and leaned against a filing cabinet. "When we were in your car, I asked you if this was your first shooting. You only said no. By your reaction, I gathered it was a sensitive topic."

He found an old-style oak office chair and cautiously tested its safety before tipping back. "It's a subject that I don't care to dwell on. But, to answer the question, it's my third."

"So, all this stuff isn't new to you?" asked Dunlap.

"Nope. But I hafta tell you one thing. It doesn't make it any easier. Those guys might be scumbags, but they're also human beings. Enough said."

Following a brief silence, Dunlap reached into her jacket pocket and pulled out a couple of her energy bars. Holding one of them out, she asked, "Want one?"

He appeared to eye it with some misgivings. "Is that one of your health food bars?"

"I suppose you could consider it one." She reached out farther. "Here, give it a try."

"Sure, what the hell. After all, you're the boss."

Relinquishing her hold, she resumed her relaxed demeanor. "Knowing you is like saying, 'This wine is fine, rather than saying this is a fine wine.'"

Munching on the bar, he mumbled, "You're one heck of a firecracker when it comes to comebacks."

"Maybe you just bring out the best in me," she said between bites.

Morris forced a smile. "Maybe. Hey, before we come to blows, do you want to take the first catnap?"

"I'm good. Tell me why you think we should be here and on this second-shift schedule."

He crumpled up the wrapper and shoved it into his leather jacket's pocket. "The captain and I figured if anything's going to happen, it was going to be at night. Also, we figured it was unlikely to occur past midnight."

"I've wanted to ask when you first mentioned it. Why midnight?"

"Any movement around Jones Island, after midnight, would arouse suspicion. The only things that move after midnight are rats."

Dunlap nodded. "Okay, but initially, you were supposed to keep an eye on Tony. Now we're doing stakeout duty on a storage locker. Why the change?"

"See, this locker and that chair hafta be really important to Tony. Let's just say that the chair is a big piece of cheese and bait for the rat, Tony."

There was a rattle of keys from below.

Morris and Dunlop rushed to the window. From their second-story position, they observed the watchman make his way past the row of storage units. Not bothering to handle each lock, the custodian simply kicked each door before moving on to the next. When he came to the last locker, he reached out and checked the lock's security before continuing around the corner, and out of their view, to the chain-link fence. Finished with the inspection, he returned to his shack.

"Note the time," Morris whispered. "We'll see if there's a pattern."

CHAPTER TWENTY-SEVEN

"Higgely Piggeldy"

"Is he dead?" asked Kyle as Adam knelt next to the motionless body of Henry Ludlow.

"He's still breathing. I think he's okay. Shit, everything is going to hell. We can't hang around here. We gotta boogie."

Kyle looked down at his midsection. "I'm bleeding," he yelled. "The bastard stabbed me with that rod."

"Quick, open your coat and lift your sweatshirt," ordered Adam. "Go, lay down on the table."

Kyle threw off his clothing from the waist up and climbed onto the table with uncharacteristic swiftness.

"Hell, sure enough, you're leaking."

"I'm sniffing the light!"

"Shut up, it ain't that bad. You ain't dying. Here, hold this scarf on your stomach while I try to find something else."

Adam hurried to the back room where he had seen the pub owner emerge when they first arrived.

"Why you lying bastard," he mumbled, gazing at the smoked ham that hung on a hook over the kitchen's worktable. He grabbed a bottle, smelled it before taking a sip, took a large swallow of the brandy, then snatched two aprons from pegs in the beam from overhead.

When Adam returned, he could see the fear in Kyle's eyes and noted his skin's paleness. "Here, drink this," he ordered.

While Kyle drank, Adam ripped off a section of cloth from one of the aprons. He took back the bottle, then poured some on the wound.

"It stings," yelled Kyle.

"It's supposed to sting."

Adam took the fragment of cloth and placed it on the gash. Using the second apron, he fashioned a bandage around Kyle's middle.

"There, that'll hold you," Adam said, taking another large swig of brandy. "The doc needs some medicine, too."

The pub owner began to stir. Moaning in pain, he made a feeble attempt to right himself but faltered.

Adam picked up the discarded poker and handed it to Kyle. "If he gets up ... you know what to do. I'll be back."

"Hey Adam, it's really smarting. How do ya expect me to do that, with me deathing?"

"Don't worry. I told you, you ain't dying. As long as he's on the ground, you're the man. Remember that."

Dashing back to the kitchen, Adam selected a knife from the workbench and promptly cut down the ham. It fell onto the bench with a thump. With equal swiftness, he cut off a section of rope. Returning to the dining area, he saw Ludlow struggling to get up.

"Not so fast," yelled Adam before kicking him back to the ground.

Still, in the grips of confusion, the pub owner tried to fight the attempt to tie him. "You're nothing but a bludger," howled Ludlow. "I'll see you hang,"

"You're gonna hafta catch us first," Adam said as he secured the last knot.

"You bloody prig. I'll get you and drag you to the salt box meself."

Adam used the remnants of the apron to muzzle him. "There," he said in triumph, "now you can yell all you want."

"How's your stomach?" asked Adam as Kyle drew closer to him.

"I feel kinda funny, and it burns. I'm ready to blow this pop-stand."

"C'mon, let's go back to the kitchen and load up some food and see what else we can find."

Taking an empty flour sack, they filled it with the ham and a loaf of bread before ransacking the rest of the kitchen.

"Whoa! What have we here?" shouted Adam.

"Whatcha got?" asked Kyle.

"A strange-looking toolie."

"Lemme see that," Kyle said as he tried to snatch it.

"Watch it," cried Adam. "You'll get us killed. You can't just grab something like this."

"Is it loaded?"

Adam aimed the gun at a wall. "Looks like it."

"Pull the trigger."

"Sure, and have anyone nearby poke around to see who made the noise?" Adam shoved the gun into his coat pocket. "C'mon, I think I saw a cash box in the cabinet where I found this six-shooter."

Adam pulled a box out and opened it on the workbench. Unlike the church's strongbox, it lacked a lock. He flipped open the lid. "Now that's a lot of dough."

From the other room, where they had left the pub owner, they heard a loud clang. Dashing to see what happened, they found Ludlow, untied, holding a log lifter. With rage in his eyes, he rushed toward them. Adam pulled the revolver from his pocket.

"Drop it, or you die," ordered Adam.

The pub owner froze.

"I said, drop it!"

Apparently weighing his chances, he remained immobile.

"Something wrong with your hearing, mister? Drop it!"

Kyle, standing near Ludlow, lashed out at him with his poker.

Recoiling from the attack, Ludlow struck Kyle's outstretched hand with his metal tool. Crying out in pain, Kyle spun backward at the same time that Adam pulled the trigger.

Nothing happened.

The pub owner rushed forward. His eyes, seething with hatred, raised the log lifter over his head. Adam staggered backward. Holding the gun in front of him, he pulled back the hammer with both thumbs. He squeezed the trigger again.

The gun barked. A stream of smoke shot out at the innkeeper.

Stunned, Ludlow checked his advance. He looked down at his chest then back at Adam before collapsing to the ground.

CHAPTER TWENTY-EIGHT

"Special Delivery"

Captain Ed Chalmers leaned back comfortably in his office chair with his hands cupped on his stomach. "Here's the thing. I want to brief you about that warehouse you're using before you go on your watch tonight. First of all, congratulations to both of you for a great job in bringing down that meth lab."

"Thanks, Captain," Morris said.

Dunlap, who had been reading the report, looked up and chimed in. "Yeah, thanks, Captain, but Detective Morris did all the heavy lifting." She gave Morris a nod.

"Well, I saw it as a team effort. Now back to the warehouse. The building has been vacant for a few years. After going into receivership, the bank took over and had been actively trying to sell it. It turns out that a bank employee used his position to lease it privately. Thanks to you two, that arrangement ended."

"Can we continue to use the place?" asked Morris.

"Short answer, yes. But I'm not sure for how long. The bank is grateful for us uncovering the lab. The guy who was running the scam actively tried to discourage any deal from going through. We are charging him as an accomplice." Chalmers reached into his desk and pulled out Morris's gun, and slid it across his desk. "I got your Glock back from ballistics."

Detective Morris removed the loaner gun from his holster and traded it with the one on the desk.

"There's one other thing," began Chalmers, "I need to tell you before you go on your watch tonight. I have to fill you in on Tony's other activity."

"What's that?" asked Morris.

"You see, Tony, deals in antiquities. At first, his interest appeared to be a hobby and legit. But now we are finding those revenues are pretty impressive. I have to admit—no one ever gave it any attention until this whole chair business."

"By impressive, do you mean huge?" asked Dunlap.

"You bet. This is what went down. Tony buys estates and sells what he can or sets up an auction."

"That doesn't sound suspicious," Dunlap said.

"You're right, but the estates he buys are usually a collection of worthless junk. Sure, once in a while, he gets lucky, but he appears to sell these odds and ends at a premium."

Morris laughed. "So, the guy has a real talent for business."

"A skunk is a skunk, is a skunk," answered Chalmers. "And Tony isn't about to change his smell, either. I now think he's stealing valuable items and blending them with marginal secondhand goods."

"So, do you think the chair is one of those high-priced artifacts?" asked Dunlap.

"That chair is involved, but I can't put my finger on it," replied Chalmers.

She nodded. "When we were watching them move it, they were holding it ever so carefully—like it was made of glass."

"Well, we're not going to solve the mystery sitting here jawing about it."

"You're right, Captain," Morris said as he began to rise.

———

Morris opened the pizza box and walked over to the warehouse window. "Go ahead, have the first slice."

The room, no longer illuminated by daylight, was now bathed in a reddish hue.

Dunlap selected a piece and slid it onto a napkin. She moved over to the desk and reoccupied her earlier position on its surface, using the file cabinet as a backrest. "This isn't going to help my figure, but thanks. I'm going to have to take a longer run tomorrow."

"You run?" he asked.

In the middle of a chew, she mumbled, "Uh-hum."

Morris set up the tripod then mounted the video camera. He looked through the camera's eyepiece, adjusted it, then turned on the power. "I should probably take up jogging, too."

"It's never too late."

He helped himself to the pizza then sat down on the desk chair. "I don't know. Getting up early in the morning, putting on some sweats, and braving the cold isn't my cup of tea." He took a large bite from the slice.

"You don't run on the first day. Matter-of-fact, you don't run in the first week. You build up to it."

"I don't know. I suppose I would hafta give up this stuff?" He raised the slice in the air before taking a bite.

"You would have to readjust your lifestyle."

"I gave up smoking years ago. That was enough adjustment for me."

"And do you feel better for it?" she asked.

"Well, yeah."

"And jogging will do the same thing—make you feel better. I'll tell you what. You come over to my place, and I'll give you the first lesson in running. What do you say?"

"I thought you said you don't run in the first week."

"You don't. I'll show you—"

There was a rattle of metal from down below. Morris shoved the remaining slice into his mouth and jumped to the window. "Nothing," he muttered, "it's only the custodian making his rounds." He began to turn away but halted. "Hey, take a look at this."

Red taillights overpowered by backup lights guided a white van to the front of the last storage unit.

Dunlap moved next to him. "This could get interesting," she said.

Cautiously peeking below, they observed an *Acme* truck come to a stop. The custodian, with keys in hand, unlocked the storage locker's door and lifted it.

Except for the chair, the truck's backup lights revealed an empty space. The driver killed the engine and moved to the rear with his co-driver following him. Guided by the watchman's flashlight beam, they lifted the vehicle's gate and proceeded to unload their cargo.

"What the hell?" exclaimed Morris.

CHAPTER TWENTY-NINE

"If Wishes Were Horses"

Unlike his dine-and-dash from the Green Hog, Adam's flight from the Golden Galleon filled him with terror as he gasped for breath. The notion of killing a second man didn't dull his conscience; it tortured him. Believing he was far enough away from the scene of his crime, he slowed down. Having used the tracks of a railroad as their escape route, he glanced back at Kyle.

"You didn't have to pop that dude," Kyle gasped.

Adam, still starving for air, paused and turned. "I didn't have a choice. He was gonna kill me. It was self-defense."

"Like that night guard?"

"Shut up. You don't know shit. If we got captured, after jackin' that church, we would have hung anyway."

"Wait up. My stomach's on fire."

Adam sat down on a nearby berm, his breath slowly returning. He called out, "C'mon, set your ass down. Let me have a look at your gut."

Kyle, appearing distraught, leaned back and undid his coat.

Adam pushed up Kyle's shirt, inspected the improvised bandage, then eased it away to look at the gash. He reached inside the sack and pulled out the bottle of brandy. He poured a little on the wound.

"Shit! That still burns, man."

"Quit your belly-aching." Adam held out the bottle. "Here, this will make it better."

Kyle leaned back and took a large gulp. Breathing out with gusto, he said, "Yeah, that makes me feel better, but how does it look?"

Adam reset the dressing. "Ah ... it looks kinda red."

"A little red, or real red, bad?"

"It's red. When we get back home, we'll have a doc look at it."

"Will we ever make it back?"

"Yeah, yeah, sure we will. Hey, we're only a couple of hours away from that mansion. We'll jump on that chair and fly home. Easy as light cheese," Adam said, helping himself to some brandy.

"Do ya know where that place is?"

"That guy on the horse said we got to go east. That sun's starting to set. So, we keep it behind us."

"Are you sure?"

"Hey, in Milwaukee, the sun rises in the east, over Lake Michigan, and sets in the west."

"Talking about horses, I wish we had a couple of them now," Kyle said.

Adam rose. "C'mon, get up. We have to get there before it gets dark."

Rising from the berm, Kyle remarked, "I see you ditched your strange-looking hat."

"Yeah, in a rush out of that place, I just forgot it. I see you left yours behind, too."

"I feel naked without it. And what happened to your Brewers cap?"

Adam reached into his coat pocket. "Shit, I forgot that one, too. We have to haul ass. Once that sun goes down, it's gonna get a lot colder."

As they followed the railroad tracks, they came upon a three-way intersection marked with a signpost.

Adam pointed. "That way says Gateshead eight and a quarter, and that Brockley Whins, one. That other one is marked Boldon, three and a quarter. I think it's pointing south."

"Didn't that hottress, the one that fingered us at the courthouse, say something about Boldon New Winning?" asked Kyle.

"Yeah, she did. Maybe they didn't have enough room on that sign to spell out the whole word? C'mon, it's close enough. Let's take a chance on that one."

Without further discussion, they began to follow the road.

"Hey, Adam."

"What?"

"If we stay on this and see someone who acts like, ya know, they know us, ain't that gonna be bad for us?"

No sooner had Kyle made his remark that a horse-drawn carriage began bearing down on them in the distance.

"Yeah, you're right. We can't take a chance. Quick, let's head for that treeline."

As soon as the carriage passed them, three more wagons followed, each with a collection of passengers. What struck Adam as curious were the occupants' festive attitude—as if they were going on a picnic.

Adam and Kyle once more followed the road but stayed along its edge. "I'm guessing we won't be able to follow this into town," Adam said. "We'll have to find some other way to get back to that house."

"Hey, Adam."

"Yeah, what?"

"That sun is gonna set, and we don't have a flashlight. What are we gonna do?"

"We need to move faster."

———

Having skirted the town under cover of twilight, they hurriedly found the road they used earlier to get into Boldon New Winning and caught sight of the mansion.

"Hey, Adam."

"What now?"

"I'm hungry. How about a slice of that ham and some bread?"

"We're almost home. Can't you wait?"

"I'm hungry, and my stomach is burning. Just a little piece of ham and bread."

"Okay, okay." Adam sat cross-legged on the ground. He opened the sack. Using the pub's knife, he cut off a couple of slices of meat and handed one to Kyle. "Here, this will hold you until we get home."

"When I get home, I'm gonna buy me a big cheeseburger and a cold beer," mumbled Kyle, his mouth stuffed with food.

"Yeah, me, too. C'mon, chew while we walk. We gotta get the hell outta here."

The sun had already set, and only its faint afterglow remained when they approached the front door of the manor. Everything was still with no evidence of human activity. Adam cautiously turned the front door's handle. He found it unlocked.

"Now, don't make a sound," he whispered. Holding the revolver he stole from the inn-keeper trained ahead, he slowly opened the door and eased himself into the foyer. The hinges squealed, and the floorboards protested as Kyle brought up the rear. Only two wall sconces lit the interior, one inside the hall and the other on the staircase wall. Closing the door with equal care, they went directly to the staircase on their right. Again, the stairs creaked beneath them. Halfway up the first landing, the entrance to the den shot opened.

There, backlighted and framed in the opened doorway, stood the short, plump form of Lord Byron Turner.

With a lantern in one hand and a sword in the other, he yelled, "You! I know you two. You're the brigands that killed the town's watchman."

Lord Turner charged toward them.

CHAPTER THIRTY

"Hocus Pocus"

"I don't get it," said Morris, relinquishing the binoculars, his voice low.

Dunlap trained the glasses on the storage locker below. "Yeah, it's not what you could call illegal stuff," she said, her speech hushed.

"Unless the stuff's stolen," responded Morris.

"I suppose, but that stuff is small potatoes compared to what you tell me about Tony and his operation. I don't understand the secrecy. I see an electric fan, a couple of car batteries, a few wire coils, and a small portable generator. Nothing that I would call illegal. Oh, one more thing—a five-gallon container of gas."

She handed the binoculars back to Morris. "Yeah, it certainly is an odd collection of things." He paused. "Remember the test where you had to identify the thing that doesn't belong?"

"Yeah?"

Morris turned away from the window and stared at Dunlap. "When you think about it, all those things fit together. The generator supplies the electricity, the battery stores the electricity, and the wires transmit the electricity."

"And the fan?"

"I don't know. Keeps you cool? But it all has to do with electricity." Morris was about to turn back but stopped. "The chair."

"What about the chair?" asked Dunlap.

"By no stretch of the imagination does the chair belong."

"Okay?"

Morris grinned. "That chair is the key, and it has something to do with that other stuff."

"Maybe Tony is going to make his own electric chair?" mocked Dunlap.

"Ha, ha. And the fan?"

"Why, keep him cool, of course."

"I'm sure that's it," he said and walked toward the open pizza box. "While you think up more outrageous ideas, keep an eye on them, but I'll have another slice."

Dunlap turned toward the window in time to see the Acme van pull away. "They're going," she said and resumed surveillance of the locker.

It wasn't until Tony arrived that she woke Morris, who chose to nap after stuffing himself with half the pie.

"Hey, Rick. It's time to earn your keep," she whispered while nudging him.

His eyes fluttered open. "Huh? How long was I out?"

"Maybe an hour. We'll dock it from your pay."

"Morris slipped off the desk and stretched in place. "What's happening?"

"Tony just showed up."

"What?"

"Yep, Tony and his driver are moving toward the locker."

Racing toward the window, he accepted the binoculars from Dunlap. Training them on the group, he observed the watchman unlock the door before pulling it open. The three of them, with Tony in the lead, moved into the storage locker. The caretaker then turned and lowered the door.

"Okay," Dunlap began, "what do you think that's all about, Rick?"

"Beats the hell out of me. Maybe they're playing three-handed canasta?"

"You are a bundle of laughs, Rick. I think I can reasonably say that they won't be using the generator in that enclosed space."

Morris shook his head. "Susan, this is by far the most interesting case I ever worked."

"I suppose any future one will be dull by comparison?"

"You can take that to the bank. And that will probably be true for you, too."

With them focused on the locker below, neither spoke a word. Finally, Morris declared, "What the hell could be so interesting that three guys confine themselves in a storage room for over an hour?"

"You're right. It's baffling, and we haven't heard any unusual sounds."

"Hey, look," Morris whispered. "The door's opening."

The watchman pushed the roll door open while Tony and his driver Stephen moved outside. Each man held a medium-sized, ornately framed painting. As they carefully loaded them into the Mercedes' trunk, the custodian promptly came to their aid. He placed a heavy blanket between the two works of art, then laid one more on top before closing the trunk.

"Where did they get those pictures?" asked Morris, training his binoculars into the interior of the storage space. "The generator, the fan, and the other stuff is gone. What the hell just happened? Are we missing something?"

Dunlap shook her head. "I saw what you saw."

Tony's chauffeured car pulled away, leaving the watchman bathed in the red glow of its taillights. Now alone, he proceeded to lock up the only thing still visible—the chair.

CHAPTER THIRTY-ONE

"Portrait of a Woman"

Captain Chalmers handed detective Rick Morris two standard-sized photocopies then returned to his desk. "They're a bit grainy, but you get the idea," he said before sitting down.

"This first one." Morris held it in the air. "The lab boys did an excellent job of blowing it up. I don't suppose they have a clue who painted it?" he said and handed the copies to Dunlap.

"No, it's too soon. After all, we just got your tape yesterday. And talking about that tape, I watched it several times and still can't get over how Tony managed to make all that stuff disappear. Do you think there might be some sort of trapdoor in the place?"

Morris shook his head. "I don't think so. From the angle of our camera, we got a clear view of the inside. With the floor being concrete, we didn't see that as a possibility. And we didn't see any indication of any other access door."

"This portrait of a woman," interrupted Dunlap, "it looks familiar. I've seen it somewhere."

"You have?" asked Chalmers, turning to her, his eyes bright with surprise.

"After completing my bachelor's degree in political science, I studied for a Master of Arts."

Morris stared at her, his mouth dropping slightly.

"I have to admit that information was in your resume, but I didn't give it much thought other than it was a master's degree," confessed Chalmers.

"I thought I would go into teaching after the military."

"Back to this picture," Chalmers began, waving it at Dunlap. "What do you know about it?"

She cleared her throat. "Okay, I think the artist is Theodor van Holst, but I don't remember the title of the work."

Chalmers dropped back into his chair. He pursed his lips before sighing. "Okay, what's so special about this painting that you should remember the artist?"

Dunlap forced a smile. "First of all, the last name of the artist, Holst, was easy to remember because of his brother Gustav Holst."

Both Morris and Chalmers gazed blankly at her.

"You know—the composer." She took in a deep breath before gradually releasing it. "Holst, the painter, was considered the link between the older English Romantic painters and ..."

She saw a glassy stare in her audience. "Well, anyway, he was a significant artist."

"Thanks for that art history lesson, but we need more current information about the artwork itself," said Chalmers. "We need to find out who owns that painting and reported it stolen."

He handed the photograph to Morris. "It's almost noon. You two go and get something to eat, then call me. In the meantime, I'll get in touch with the Milwaukee Art Museum and find out who is their resident expert on—"

"European art," chimed Dunlap.

"Yeah, European art." Chalmers jotted down a note. "I'll set up the appointment for you two. Hopefully, you'll get to see someone today."

———

"Do you want to walk off that steak sandwich or drive to the art museum?" asked Dunlap as she and Morris left the *State Street Bistro*.

"I suppose the correct answer is to walk, but that means we hafta walk back."

"The answer is yes. And I think a brisk walk will be good for you. Besides, this could be the beginning of your workout program."

"Okay, lead on," he said, motioning agreement with a gloved hand.

Dunlap finished buttoning her tan leather car coat, then adjusted the faux fur collar, before setting a robust pace, toward Lake Michigan.

"Do you always walk this fast?" asked Morris, who trailed slightly.

"This is nothing compared to my workout pace. I can see you'll be needing special attention."

"I thought we were going to be taking a stroll to the museum?"

"No, I said 'brisk walk,' not a stroll."

"I thought this was going to be fun," Morris said with a slight wheeze.

"Okay, considering your age and weight, I'll ease up a bit."

"Very funny." He quickened his stride and began taking the lead.

"Okay, you can slow up. I don't want you to have a heart attack."

He eased up and matched her stride. "You are right about me being out of shape. Years of bad food choices and sitting on stakeouts takes a toll on the body."

"Rick, I am serious about helping you get back into shape. Starting tomorrow, why don't you stop by my place a couple of hours before our next shift. We'll go on a forced march together."

Morris grinned. "Forced march? Sounds like fun."

"Don't let the title put you off. It will be fun," she said, finishing with a smile.

For the following few blocks, neither spoke.

"By the way," Morris finally said, "why didn't you go into teaching?"

Her smile faded. "That plan died when Tim died. Maybe it was retribution for the murder that I decided to go into law enforcement. For me, it didn't make a difference whether the criminal was in Afghanistan or Atlanta. My new cause was justice."

"I have to admit you are a fine officer. I think you would have made a great teacher, too."

"Thanks, but you're making me blush." She picked up the tempo.

When they reached the museum, they entered through the central vestibule, then made their way down a long archway to the offices.

Morris craned his neck as they traveled down the lengthy portico. "Wow, it's beautiful."

"Don't tell me you've never been here before?"

"Not inside."

"The architect is Santiago Calatrava."

"Didn't he play for the Miami Marlins?"

"You're impossible." She pointed to the office directory. "Paul Bender, Director of European Art."

Morris pushed the elevator's call button. "I'm glad we won't have to walk up any stairs."

Dunlap forced a laugh. "I know you're not serious. Try not to embarrass me when we talk about art. Okay?"

"Hey, it's your bag. I'll let you do all the talking," Morris said, his hands opened in submission.

The door to the office of Paul Bender was open. On the small side, his art print cluttered walls made the room claustrophobic. When they entered, Bender rose to greet them. "And you two must be Detective Morris and Officer Dunlop."

Following the round of handshakes, Paul Bender took his seat and offered his visitors a place to sit. "Your Captain Chalmers informed me that you have a painting that requires my services," he said, followed with a soft smile.

"Yes, I have a copy of it on my cellphone," Dunlap said as she reached inside her coat pocket.

Morris appeared detached from the exchange, focusing his attention on the print-covered room. "You have a lot of stuff on your walls," he said.

"Yes, *that stuff*, as you call it, are the examples of centuries of creative endeavors by the world's greatest artists."

"Hah, you don't say?"

"Here it is," said Dunlap, reaching over the desk and the same time giving Morris a sideways glance of disapproval.

Cupping the phone in both hands, he studied the image. He tsked.

"Oh, yes, *The Wish* by Theodor von Holst. He was quite eccentric—preferring to paint the demonic or erotic. Of course, that put him outside the taste of most people of that era. By some, he is considered a link between English Romantic painters such as William Blake and Pre-Raphaelite circles, such as John Everett Millais." He handed the phone back to Dunlap.

"That is very interesting, but do you know who owns the painting?" she asked, returning the phone to her pocket.

"By the image on your phone, I should think you already know that."

"We're not certain if that's the rightful owner of the work," answered Dunlap. "We suspect it's either a copy of the painting or evidence of a theft."

He laughed. "To know the owner of every painting in the world would be quite a feat." Ignoring his desk computer, he swiveled his chair around to the back counter and opened another monitor. After several clicks of his mouse and fingering of the keyboard, he said, "Hmm. It appears it was in a private collection."

"Was?" asked Dunlap.

"Yes, the owner was an art critic, Brian Sewell."

Dunlap jotted down the name in her notebook. "And what happened to him?" She looked up, waiting for the reply.

"He died several years ago, in 2015."

CHAPTER THIRTY-TWO

"How Many Miles to Babylon?"

"Stop right there!" shouted Adam, "or I'll fill you full of lead."

Lord Byron Turner, his sword aimed up at Adam, glanced down. Seeing the gun, he froze midstride.

Adam cautiously walked down the steps and faced Turner. "Who else is here?" he demanded.

Turner, still holding his sword, retreated slightly.

"Listen, mister. You ran your mouth off in the courthouse easy enough when you fingered us. Now spill the beans. Who else is here?"

"Spill the beans?" he asked in apparent puzzlement.

"Yeah, tell me if anyone is in this house besides you. And drop the blade."

"Where did you get that thing in your hand?"

"Never mind, where I got it. Now drop the blade, or I'll show you what this thing can do."

Lord Turner flung the rapier sword aside. It trundled over several times before coming to rest against the wall.

"Go get it, Kyle," ordered Adam.

Bending over to retrieve the sword, Kyle grabbed his stomach and groaned.

"Okay, mister, let's get back into your man cave," Adam said while coaxing Turner toward his study.

Several wall sconces illuminated the interior of Lord Turner's study, supplemented with two oil lanterns. Lord Turner, leading the way, stopped at his desk and placed the lantern he held on its surface.

"Okay, pal, that's far enough," Adam commanded. "Now go over to that chair." He motioned toward an ornately carved armchair in front of the desk. "Go on, sit down."

While keeping his gun trained on Turner, Adam went and took his place on another imposing chair behind the desk. As he opened each drawer, and between hurried glances at Turner, he inquisitively rummaged through their contents. Finished probing the desk's interior, an ornate letter opener on its surface caught Adam's attention. He picked it up, felt its weight, and slipped it into his coat pocket. "Nice place you got here," he said while eyeing the walls adorned with paintings and other curiosities.

Kyle sat in an overstuffed chair near the fireplace, lazily waving his newly acquired sword in the air. He held the other hand to his stomach. His movements were stilted—he appeared uncomfortable.

"Who are you, and by what means did you arrive in my manor?" asked Lord Turner.

"You were in that courthouse. You heard we're from Milwaukee. Why you asking?

"Well, poor fellow, I had misgivings about you. Later, I began to deliberate if you were associates of Mr. Anthony Angelo. Are you acquainted with him?"

Adam perked up. His propensity for self-adulation kicked in. "Yeah, we're pals. Why do you ask?"

"Then, you came through the chair, didn't you?"

Adam glanced at Kyle, then Turner. "What of it?

Turner opened his arms in a gesture of welcoming. "I'm afraid I've done you, two gentlemen, a disservice. When my gatekeeper reported of your presence, I immediately sent word to the local constabulary. I now regret my actions."

"Where's the gatekeeper, now?" asked Adam.

"News came of a great fire in Gateshead. Having been informed of the numerous deaths and loss of property, I sent my staff to offer aid, including the house nurse."

Adam rose and moved to the front of the desk. Leaning against it, still holding the gun in one hand, he folded his arms and said, "We were there. It's a total cluster."

"Cluster?"

"It's a mess. We were lucky to leg it before we got our asses fried."

"Sir, your Christian name is Adam, is it not?" asked Lord Turner.

"Yeah, my handle is Adam Cabano, and my wingman is Kyle Kraft. You were there. That's what we told the judge."

"What's a wingman?"

"You know, my co-pilot—like on an airplane."

"Airplane? What's an airplane?"

Adam stretched out his arms. "It flies in the air."

"Oh, a flying machine. I have heard of such things. Sir George Cayley called his a glider."

"Yeah, whatever," Adam scoffed.

"Do all the people in this village of Milwaukee talk like you?"

Adam raised his head in amusement and laughed. "Only the cool ones."

"Cool ones?"

"Yeah, the Steve McQueens."

"Are these McQueens a prominent family in the village of Milwaukee?"

"Never mind. It's just an expression, like, this place sucks."

"Well, Mr. Cabano, you are the first person to arrive here using that chair. I see you weren't hurt."

"Yeah, it's quite a ride."

"My stomach," Kyle called out, "it's really burning,"

Lord Turner directed his attention to Kyle. "What's ails your associate?"

"Someone stuck a poker in his gut."

"Maybe I can be of some assistance? Do you want me to attend to your friend? I may be able to lessen the pain."

"We were going to split when you busted us."

"You are free to go, but allow me to tend to your friend first. I want to learn more about Milwaukee and all the wonders of the future. I assure you, Mr. Cabano, that your acceptance will have monetary rewards."

Adam considered the offer. He watched Kyle, the sword no longer in his hand, squirm uncomfortably in his chair. He waved the revolver at Turner. "Yeah, but no funny stuff."

Lord Turner got to his feet and moved toward a cabinet on the far side of the room. Adam followed, keeping a close watch. Turner opened the doors to the cupboard then withdrew a tiny corked bottle and small crock. Taking the containers to Kyle, he said, "Let me have a look at that injury."

Kyle removed his coat and fatigue jacket, then lifted his shirt.

"My word," Turner exclaimed, "it is indeed an angry wound." He moved to a side table where a basin and pitcher lay. He soaked a cloth with water, then returned to Kyle's side and washed the gash. After drying the wound, he poured a thick yellow substance on the injury.

"What's that stuff?" asked Adam.

"Honey, directly from my hives. It will help heal it."

Setting the honey aside, Turner uncorked the bottle and offered it to Kyle. "Take a sip, lad. It will ease the pain."

"What is it?" asked Kyle, reaching out.

"It's laudanum. It will reduce the pain, and your associate will be a little unsteady. He will undoubtedly fall into a slumber."

"But we have to get back home," Adam said. "You know what they said in court. They're gonna hang us."

"Rest assured, my dear man, you will be safe. No one will know of your presence here."

Having hesitated during the exchange, Kyle accepted the bottle and took a sip before handing it back.

Turner slipped the bottle into his coat pocket and handed Kyle a clean cloth. "Here, put this on your stomach, then follow me," he said. Taking a lantern off the side table, he held out a helping hand and guided Kyle into an adjoining room. Small and cluttered, the room contained a makeshift bed, surrounded by numerous electronic apparatuses. Without hesitation, Kyle sat down, rolled over onto the divan, and closed his eyes. Turner took a blanket off a nearby chest and covered him. "There, that should hold you." He went and left him in the darkened room.

Upon leaving, Adam thought the room resembled something from a Frankenstein movie. He followed Turner back into the library. There, a disheveled man waited. The man, wearing an open three-quarter-length coat, with baggy trousers and scuffed boots, stood next to the desk. Cradled in his arms, he held a shotgun, its barrel pointing toward the ground. His eyes lit up, and he came to attention.

Adam stiffened as well and instinctively pointed his gun at him. "Who's that?"

"That's Lawrence, my gatekeeper."

"You said you sent everyone away," Adam said his gun-hand trembling.

No one moved. The tension rising, Lord Turner slowly reached over and gently persuaded Adam to lower his weapon. "I told you I sent my staff to Gateshead, not my gatekeeper. Now, sir, let us have a drink together. I want to know more about your world and our associate Mr. Anthony Angelo."

Lawrence retreated to a corner of the room. Sitting down on a worn fiddleback chair, he cradled the shotgun across his lap while his eyes remained fixed on Adam.

CHAPTER THIRTY-THREE

"Long Slow Distance"

Susan Dunlap bounded down the few concrete steps in front of her eastside apartment building to greet Rick Morris as he exited his Subaru Forester.

"Ready to go?" she asked while running in place.

Morris leisurely walked around the front of the vehicle. He wore gray sweat pants, a matching sweatshirt embroidered with a Milwaukee Police Department logo, and nondescript tennis shoes.

"Those are some pretty fancy running clothes," he said, eyeing Dunlap in her two-piece tracksuit.

"Yea...ahhh, and you're sporting some pretty remarkable running togs yourself. Academy issue?"

"Yep, they never go out of style."

"Well, let's get on with it." She zipped up her body-hugging thermal top. "The first thing you want to do is stretch those muscles. Watch me and follow my lead."

After their warm-up, Dunlap set an average pace as they began fast-walking along Milwaukee's eastside's neighborhood streets. "This will get your blood flowing," she said, outdistancing Morris by a few feet.

"This is a little faster than our walk to the museum yesterday."

"Yep, that was, like you said, walking, and this is speed walking. We'll get to power walking eventually."

"And then running, right?" Morris asked.

"Don't worry—we'll get there. A few weeks of this, and then we start the real fun stuff, the LSD training." She smiled broadly.

"Ah, I'm sure you're thinking of something different when you say LSD training than I am."

"You're right. LSD training means long, slow distance training."

"And that is?"

"We start by doing some practice runs. You know, I'll set up a practice race, but at a slower pace. The distance will be the same. Only the speed will change. Now let's get moving."

When they returned to the starting point, Morris grabbed his sides. He bent forward, gulping in air. "How many miles did we travel?" he gasped.

"Only two."

"Seems like more."

"We have one more thing to do."

"What's that?"

"Stretching. We need to stretch those muscles. C'mon, this is the easy part."

Finished with the cooldown, Morris started for his car. "I'm ready for a hot shower and a nap."

"Rick, hold up. Why don't you come up to my place for a cup of tea?"

Morris turned and nodded. "Sure, sounds like a great idea, although I'm not what you would call a tea drinker."

"Well, it's time I help broaden your horizons."

Dunlap unlocked the front door of her apartment building and checked her mailbox. "Sometimes the mailman is early," she said, closing the empty box.

"Mailman?"

"Yeah, the *mailman*. If he were a she, I'd say mail lady. I call 'em by the way I see 'em. You're not one of them word-police people, are you?"

"No, not at all. I'm only surprised."

"Because I'm a liberated woman, working in a progressive society with its strict rules of behavior and speech?"

"Frankly, yeah."

"You have a lot to learn about me, Rick. Ready for a climb?"

"Third floor, right?"

"How'd you guess?"

"Well, your mailbox said 301, for starters. And the fact I just finished a two-mile forced march seems almost a given."

Dunlap laughed before sprinting up the stairs.

"Pardon the mess," she said while opening the door. "I usually straighten things up after my run."

"It can't be as bad as my place," he said, huffing. "I tidy up *before* the start of each season—at the same time, I change my wardrobe."

Small and cozy, Dunlap's apartment was a mixture of modern, accented with ornate artwork.

"I'm sure it may seem odd to have selected those painting for my walls. I like the simplicity of modern Danish furnishings but love the elegance of the Baroque era art and its dramatic use of light."

"Yeah, I see what you mean. Maybe you can come over to my place sometime and see my collection of Elvis-on-velvet art."

"You don't strike me as a Presley *aficionado*," said Dunlap. She removed her tennis shoes.

Morris followed her lead and undid his shoes.

"Sit anywhere you feel comfortable while I make us some tea. Does oolong sound okay?"

Morris shrugged.

"I'll warn you. It has caffeine if you plan on taking a nap before our shift tonight."

She moved into the kitchenette, took a stainless-steel tea kettle, and filled it with water. "But it also has antioxidants if you're into health foods, which I'm guessing you're not."

"I wouldn't know an antioxidant if it bit me in the ass," quipped Morris while sitting down on a mist-gray, walnut trimmed lounge chair.

"Sometimes, I don't know if you're joking or serious when you say the things you do. After all, from what I have observed, you appear to be a pretty sharp detective."

"Why, because of my Sherlock Holmes talent to deduce what floor you live on?"

"No, maybe it is your sharp wit and your self-effacing character," Dunlap said. She moved to the couch facing him.

"Well, before this praise goes to my head and I become difficult to live with, I want to talk about our stakeout tonight."

Dunlap chuckled. "Like what?"

"Okay, usually on this type of surveillance, it's pretty straightforward. We keep an eye on the perp, take notes, follow, and sometimes use video. Considering the situation, I mean the fact that it was a dead-end location, who would have guessed something weird was going on behind closed doors."

"I'm assuming you have a plan?"

"If they close that door again, I want to know what they're saying. Normally we'd plant a listening device or get a court order to tap a line. Obviously, we can't get into the locker without arousing suspicion, and I'm pretty sure they don't have a phonebooth in there."

"Which leaves a parabolic listening device as the only option?" Dunlap asked.

"Hey, nothing like trying to steal my thunder."

"I only assumed that because we used similar devices in Afghanistan."

"Well, it looks like I'm gonna have to burst your bubble."

"What do you mean?"

"That kind of apparatus isn't as practical as the shotgun microphone, which has a range of 300 feet, versus a hundred with the parabolic one. Also, its noise filtering is better. And I know there are more sophisticated types, but I prefer the shotgun mic."

The teapot began to whistle.

Dunlap returned to the stove and poured the hot water over the premeasured tea into the ceramic teapot's infuser. She set a timer for four minutes.

"You make tea like a chemist," Morris said when she returned to the couch.

"Tea is a serious business for true lovers of the beverage."

"This is all new to me—being a coffee drinker myself. Now, getting back to listening during our stakeout, unfortunately, we are limited to the number of hours we can be there. So, it's a crapshoot. But I'm convinced we've picked the right time. The problem remains. We don't have a clue regarding the frequency of the visits."

"So, it's all up to us?" asked Dunlap.

He nodded. "Yeah, we'll continue to use the auto-record when we're not there. But so far, it's all normal day-to-day stuff. The sound from the inside is a new wrinkle we didn't expect."

"And there isn't another person, in the whole department, that Captain Chalmers can trust to be on-site and record when we aren't there?"

Morris shook his head. "He doesn't want to risk Tony finding out. It's that simple. And when the shit finally hits the fan, he wants boots on the ground when it does."

"I'm assuming you either have the device, or you're going to pick it up?"

"After my daily dose of antioxidants, I'm going to stop by supply and get it."

"Sounds good. And I think our tea is about ready," Dunlap said as she sprung up.

CHAPTER THIRTY-FOUR

"Paper, or Plastic?"

Lord Turner finished pouring a round of brandy before sitting at his desk. Lawrence, the gatekeeper, overlooked in the sharing, rested his shotgun against a nearby corner of the room. Adam studied him with apprehension before removing his outer coat and shoving the pistol into his peacoat.

Turner began, "Mr. Cabano, now tell me of the wonders of the future and your associate Mr. Angelo."

Adam took a sip of his drink. "Before I get into the nitty-gritty of our operation, what are you doing with all that electrical stuff?"

"In the future, did you ever hear of Joseph Swan?"

"Can't say I have."

"Hum," mused Turner. "He is a friend of mine and quite a gifted inventor. I would think his inventions would have made a significant contribution to your society."

"I'm more into buying and selling stuff."

"Like importing and exporting?"

Adam nodded. "Yeah, yeah, sorta like that."

"To answer your question, I have to relate how I acquired the chair. Like yourself, I am an importer and exporter of fine goods. During one of my many voyages to France, I happened to stay in the town of Vendée. Are you familiar with that location?"

"Uh-uh," replied Adam, shaking his head and feeling uncomfortable by his ignorance.

"I understand. Most Americans are unfamiliar with European geography. That region of France is located on the Bay of Biscay, south of Brittany. Most remarkably, it is noted for an insurrection against the revolutionary French government. While there, I happened upon a merchant who pressed upon me the prospect of possessing a chair once used by General Turreau. Does that name sound familiar, Mr. Cabano?"

Again, Adam shook his head. He took a gulp of his brandy.

"I have to confess. I was intrigued by the prospect of owning something from a notable personage, especially one with such a sordid past. I won't bore you with the horrific details of his actions during the uprising. But I will relate one incident, in particular, which, by way of the merchant's narrative, I became acquainted with the history of the chair."

Adam drained the last of his drink. He examined the gatekeeper, finding the man's silence and unrelenting scrutiny unnerving.

"I see you've finished your drink, Mr. Cabano. Let me remedy that," Lord Turner said as he reached for the bottle. After filling the glass, he topped off his own, then settled back into his chair.

Adam took a sip and nodded his approval.

"Where was I? Oh, yes, the merchant's story. General Turreau would hold court, of sorts. He made his decrees from that very chair, passing death sentences on the inhabitants of Vendée. One day, a woman whose husband had been killed through drowning on the general's orders came before him, ostensibly to receive the same fate. Seeing her, he was struck by her beauty and forced himself upon her. Infuriated by his lascivious behavior and his responsibility for her husband's death, she cursed him, saying that he would never find peace or receive the glory he so desired."

"So, what happened to her?" Adam asked before taking a sip of his drink.

"He drew his sword and killed her on the spot."

"And the dude with the chubby, what happened to him?"

"You mean the general?"

"Yep, the big cheese," Adam answered.

"After the revolution, during the Bourbon Restoration, he spent a year in prison. Then through a series of unusual circumstances, he became the ambassador to the United States."

"Well, the dude made out in the end," Adam said. "Sounds like the 'pox on you' didn't take."

"That may be somewhat debatable," Lord Turner replied. "He was abusive toward his wife. His attacks on her were thunderous and noticed by neighbors. Yet, despite his political setbacks and military failures, he was awarded the cross of Saint-Louis."

"Hey, that doesn't sound like a loser to me."

"He died before receiving it at the official ceremony," Lord Turner said.

"Oh," exclaimed Adam. Then after a moment of reflection, he asked, "Okay, what has all this stuff have to do with the *Star Trek* tele-porter chair?"

"Mr. Cabano, you have the most unusual way of expressing yourself. What's a *Star Trek* tele-porter?"

"It's something that the crew of the Enterprise uses," Adam said. But seeing the confusion on Lord Turner's face, he added, "It would take too long to extrapolate. It's sorta like what the chair does—only in outer space."

"Your people actually travel into the heavens?"

"Yep, and on the moon, too."

Lord Turner fell back into his chair. "I am a good deal shocked by your audacious claim and find such revelation hard to believe."

"It's bona fide, man. C'mon, tell me more about the chair. How'd you start shopping in the future?"

"Perhaps, I should ask you, my good man, the same question?"

Adam reached for his drink and took a gulp. "Ah, my boss, Tony Angelo, never told me. It was sorta his secret. We put stuff on it, and the stuff disappeared."

"Not knowing what would happen to you or your associate, Mr. Kroft, what made you attempt such a risk?"

"Like most things in this world, cha-ching—money," answered Adam. "Now tell me how you started doing this chair-mart stuff? Kyle and I came in after the whole shop-by-teleportation started. We just did what the boss told us to do."

"Originally, that chair was in this room. One day, a glass orb appeared on its seat. Extending from this sphere was a strange, screw-like protrusion, the likes of nothing I had ever seen. I picked it up and began to examine it. I was surprised by its lightness, and it slipped out of my hand and fell back onto the chair. To my amazement, it disappeared. I thought my eyes had deceived me. Believing the hallucination a product of the hour's lateness and a manifestation of my mind and the wine, I decided to retire. Then, remarkably, it reappeared."

"Did the chair feel electrical?" asked Adam.

"I was indeed familiar with the sensation, having been acquainted with it through my friend, Joseph Swan. Out of curiosity, I dropped a book onto the chair, and to my amazement, it disappeared. Owing to the late hour and lack of a full moon by which to travel at night, I waited until the next day to inform Joseph of my discovery. I must confess I was so excited it was with great difficulty that I was able to fall asleep."

Adam retrieved his drink and downed its contents. Ignoring the frowns of the gatekeeper, he asked, "How about another fill?"

Without hesitation, Lord Turner obliged. He poured Adam a healthy ration before refreshing his own and continued. "When I was able to show Joseph my discovery, he was wild with excitement. Trying to find out more information about the nature and source of the exchange, we added messages. Once we realized we were communicating with someone from the future, through a mutual agreement, we consented to barter with whoever was on the other end."

"So, it doesn't sound like that chair has any kind of curse attached to it," said Adam.

"I have not revealed everything, Mr. Cabano. It wasn't until later that I discovered I made a contract with a devil.

CHAPTER THIRTY-FIVE

"Let's Make a Deal"

"Mr. Cabano, is Anthony Angelo an honorable man?" asked Lord Turner.

The question struck Adam as strange. He only knew Tony Angelo by reputation. "What do you mean by honorable?"

"Is he respectable?"

"There's a lot of people in Milwaukee that respect him. Actually, I don't know anyone who would cross him."

The gatekeeper got up from his perch and moved toward the fireplace. Taking a few small logs, he laid them on the dying embers. Using bellows, he revived the flames.

Adam kept a watchful eye on him until he resumed his place in the corner of the room.

"Mr. Cabano, what I mean to ask, is Mr. Angelo a criminal?"

Adam shifted uneasily in his chair. "He's like an Al Capone kinda guy—a made-man. He's the big cheese in Milwaukee."

"Your description does puzzle me, but I think I understand the meaning. What I am about to reveal may surprise you."

Adam gulped his brandy.

"As our system of barter continued, I received a very unusual delivery. Although I said it was unusual, I probably should have said it was most unexpected. The delivery was the remains of a murdered man. Although at that moment, my gatekeeper or I didn't suspect foul play."

His voice quaking, Adam asked, "What did you do with it?"

"Acting on impulse, thinking the man sustained some injury in transit, Lawrence and I tried to revive him. Then, seeing the wound, we realized he had been murdered. At the time, we had little choice but to bury him."

Adam felt an empty feeling in the pit of his stomach. He avoided looking at Lord Turner. Instead, he stared at the fireplace, which was fully ablaze. Adam stole a sidelong glance at the gatekeeper then back at Turner, waiting for him to say something.

After a prolonged silence, Turner said, "It wasn't the last body, either."

Adam nervously considered his empty glass.

"I'm sorry, Mr. Cabano, let me fill your drink."

Adam noted the brandy level in the decanter and how it had significantly shrunk since they began their chat. With Lord Turner's back to him, he observed what appeared to be the unsteadiness of his arm as he filled Adam's glass.

"My good man," Turner began as he held out the drink with a steady hand. "I suppose you are wondering why I am telling you this?"

Again, Adam thought silence the best answer. He checked his pocket, nervously reassuring himself he had the revolver. He eyed the gatekeeper. His arms rested on his knees and leaned forward like an animal ready to pounce.

Lord Turner rubbed the back of his neck. "Over the next two years, I received three more bodies." He paused. "Out of fear of discovery by one of my household members, I had the chair moved to the attic. You said that you don't think there is a curse associated with that chair. Mr. Cabano, the real curse is what that chair makes people do. I want it to stop. Yet the intoxication of its power has me imprisoned."

Adam nodded.

"Besides, if I told Mr. Angelo of my intention to quit this endeavor, I fear for my own life. Now, knowing of your association with the chair, I was hoping you could assist me in disposing of it."

"Why do you think I would want to do that?"

"With the prospect of meeting your end at the gallows, my good man, I would think you would be most eager. I guess that you, too, have been touched by the curse."

"Why don't you just kill it?" asked Adam.

Turner smiled. "Your choice of words is interesting. I had considered that as a solution. When I touched the chair, it threw me back. It was as if it were alive and knew my thoughts."

"Hey, what about that Joseph guy? How does he feel about being a party to murder, you know, ditching those bodies in your backyard?"

"He doesn't know the full extent of my arrangement with Mr. Angelo," said Turner. "For his own good and my privacy, I have kept that a secret."

"So, only you and your gatekeeper know that part of your deal?"

The gatekeeper, no longer leaning forward, but resting back with his arms folded across his chest, looked up.

"Yes," said Turner, who then glanced over to his shotgun-wielding accomplice, giving him a nod.

Adam began to feel the brandy's effects and the lateness of the hour. He reached for his drink. The room seemed to move. Using the time to mull over the deal in his mind, he slowly sipped his brandy. "I got an idea of how we both can score a big one on this."

"Score? What do you mean by score?"

Adam leaned forward. "I want to get back to my own time, but I want to go back with some loot. You know, cash."

"What did you have in mind?" asked Lord Turner.

"I had an uncle who collected coins. Once, he found a quarter that was worth a few hundred bucks."

"I assume bucks means some sort of money in your time?"

"Yep. What I'm thinking, you give me some of your loose change, call it a payment to rid yourself of the curse. I'll make sure the problem goes away on the other side."

"It does, indeed, sound simple enough, but I have one request."

"Spill it," Adam said.

"I want to go back with you. If only for a day, I want to see the wonders of the future."

"I can make it happen," answered Adam, confident his economic situation just turned in his favor.

CHAPTER THIRTY-SIX

"Night Watch"

Detective Morris, halfway into his shift, double-checked the connections to the surveillance camera and shotgun mic.

"Just because you haven't heard anything doesn't mean it's broken," Officer Dunlap said.

"I know. I'm just tired of sitting around doing nothing and waiting for something to happen."

"Before starting your exercise program with me, you were content with eating pizzas and taking a nap."

"Yeah, in the nearly two weeks, I've lost ten pounds and been more watchful of what I eat."

"So, you have to admit, I've been a positive influence in your life," Dunlap said.

Morris smiled and sat on the desk near the window. "Yeah, yeah, but now I have to start shopping for new clothes."

"Take no offense, but you needed a wardrobe change."

"None taken." He leaned back against a file cabinet—arms crossed over his chest.

"By the way," Dunlap began, "I got a call back from the auction house on the painting by Holst."

"Who?"

"The artist who painted *The Wish*."

"What about him?"

"First of all, when Sewell died—"

"Wait, who the hell is Sewell?"

"Boy, you are exasperating. Sewell owned the painting, and when he died, the collection went up for auction.

"Oh, yeah, I forgot about him. I didn't think he was that important to the case."

"He isn't, but it turns out that a private collector bought it. It's common practice for buyers of fine art to keep their transactions secret. The long and short of it is we cannot confirm if it's still in possession of the new collector."

"So, we don't know if Tony stole the painting because no one has reported it stolen. Is that it?"

"Yeah." Dunlap zipped up her down-filled coat. "I wish this place had more heat than that space heater gives off."

"Be glad this place has electricity. Not all of my stakeouts have been this luxurious."

"Speaking of stakeouts, what do you think will happen to me after this assignment?" asked Dunlap.

"I don't know. The chief could reassign you to another detective, or he could punish me and make you my partner."

"Rick, you just said I've been a positive influence in your life."

"Yeah, I did say that, didn't I?"

"Yes, you did."

"Did you just hear that?" asked Morris.

"Hear what?"

Morris sprung from his roost and moved toward the window. He looked down at the storage locker. "Everything normal, but I could swear I heard something."

Dunlap stood beside Morris.

"There, now did you hear that?" he asked.

Dunlap nodded. "Yeah, something or someone is in that locker!"

CHAPTER THIRTY-SEVEN

"Back to the Future"

Adam's head throbbed as he began to awaken. The room was unfamiliar, and he didn't remember how he got there. Squinting beneath the wave of sunlight that streamed through the exposed windows, he surveyed his surroundings. The four-poster bed, in which he lay, included sheer drapes drawn back and tied to each post.

Fully clothed except for his peacoat and shoes, he rolled out of bed and placed his stockinged feet onto the wood floor. Cradling his head in his hands, he felt queasy, followed by the urge to relieve himself. He rose and shuffled his way to the only door and tried to open it. Finding it locked, he frantically searched for something to use as a urinal. At the foot of the bed, he spotted an ornate Wedgewood chamber pot.

After taking care of his immediate needs, he once more tried the door, but more forcibly. Finding it unbudgeable, he walked to the windows. From his second-floor perch, which overlooked the grounds below, he observed what he believed to be a stable boy leading one of the horses into the paddock. He considered opening a window and shouting to the lad but thought better of it. Instead, he remembered the skeleton key tucked away in his coat.

Before he could retrieve the key, Adam heard the clanking of metal from outside his room. There was a shuffling noise before Lord Byron Turner entered and dressed much as he had been last night. He appeared cheerful with his high-waisted pants, held in place with broad suspenders and a matching vest that bulged at his midriff.

"I assumed you would be thirsty and a bit hungry," Turner said, holding a tray with a teapot and plate of tartlets. He placed the fare on a side table. "You have to excuse me for locking the room. For your own safety, I couldn't allow you to wander about unattended."

"Where's Kyle?"

"Your friend, or as you said, your wingman, is still recovering in my storage room. I checked on him before coming here. He appears to be doing fine. Though, I believe he will need a couple more days of rest before he is fit to travel."

Adam went over to the tray and scooped up one of the small pie-shaped treats. He popped the whole confection into his mouth

"The strawberry is my favorite," admitted Turner as he poured Adam a cup of tea.

With his mouth full, Adam nodded his approval. Taking the cup, he blew on the hot tea and took a sip. "Do you have any sugar?" he mumbled.

"Mr. Cabano, in England, we take our tea unsweetened, alternating between bites of pastries and sips of tea."

The criticism touched a nerve with Adam. "Well, that's not the way I drink my hot stuff in the future," he snapped.

"I apologize, Mr. Cabano. I meant no slight by my remark."

"Ah, forget it." Adam took a sip and grabbed another tart. "Hey, first you said all your staff left. Then you tell me your gatekeeper is still hanging around. Now I looked outside before you came in, and I saw a kid pulling a horse. Who's the kid?"

"That's Lawrence's son, Oliver."

"So, does he have a mother?" asked Adam with a tinge of sarcasm in his tone.

"Oliver's mother made the pastry you find so delicious."

"Okay, how many people are on this dude ranch right now?" asked Adam directly, feeling deceived by Turner's apparent economy with the truth.

Turner did not immediately answer but walked over to the window and appeared preoccupied. "Besides myself, three, all of whom I have now made known to you."

"You said all your household went to Gateshead. When do you think they'll return?"

With his back to Adam, he said, "I received word this morning, by way of a messenger, that my staff will be assisting the injured for at least a week."

Turner turned and faced Adam. "Do you remember what we talked about last night?"

Adam, examining the remaining tart, said, "Yeah, you want to lift into the future on that magic chair."

"Considering the absence of my household staff and the condition of your friend, I believe we can make the journey two days from now."

"Sure, sure. I'm down with that." Adam picked up another tartlet.

"And you wanted nothing more than some coins in the trade?"

"That's okay with me."

Turner smiled and proceeded toward the door. "My gatekeeper's wife has prepared freshly baked bread, boiled eggs, and slices of that ham you brought. And if you need to use the privy, it is at the end of the garden."

"What's a privy?"

"We used to call it the shed."

"You mean an outhouse?"

"I suppose you could call it that, Mr. Cabano."

"You don't have any running water in this place?"

"Mr. Cabano, this is an ancient estate, and only recently have I undertaken to make changes. If it's bathing you require, I do have a bathing room on the ground floor."

Adam sniffed at his armpit. "Yeah, thanks, maybe after I get some food in me. I know I stink after spending time in that cell and back-packing all over the countryside."

Lord Turner nodded and left.

Still, only in his stockinged feet, Adam went to the side of the bed and retrieved his tennis shoes. Setting them aside next to a chair, he first checked his peacoat. Satisfied that his revolver was still in his possession, he put on his shoes and thought about spending his treasure when he returned to his own time.

"Maybe I'll buy me a yacht," he said to the empty room as he slipped on his shoes.

CHAPTER THIRTY-EIGHT

"A Fall into a Ditch Makes You Wiser"

The sun had already set as Adam and Kyle gathered around Turner's desk.

"I trust you find the sum sufficient," Lord Turner said as he pushed the pile of money in their direction.

Adam scooped up the coins and divided them between his two coat pockets.

"Hey, man!" exclaimed Kyle. "How about sharing some of that *dinero* with me?"

"Don't worry, *man*. When we get home, I'll split it with you," Adam said, patting his pockets.

"No way and no how, *man*. I want some scratch now."

"Listen, *pal*. I've taken care of you so far. Don't you trust me?"

"No, I don't," shot Kyle as he pushed himself clear from his chair and away from the desk. "Don't do me! You and your unlimited bullshit disorder. I've been screwed up the ying-yang ever since we came into this weird world. I'm exhaustipated. I'm outa here." He started for the exit. As he neared the door, he turned and yelled, "See ya on the other side, *pal*."

Adam scrambled to intercept Kyle before he touched the doorknob. "Okay, okay," he said. Fumbling into his pocket, he pulled out several coins and held them out to Kyle while grabbing him by the arm. "Here, take this. Consider it a down payment.

"No!" Kyle yelled. He pulled away and pointed. "I want everything in that pocket, or I go time diving by myself."

Floored by Kyle's reaction, Adam was about to reprimand his friend but held back. "Okay, you win." He again reached into his pocket, pulling out the rest of the coins. "Now come back, and we'll talk about our plan."

With hands outstretched, Kyle accepted the monies and swiftly transferred them into his own pockets.

Turner, standing at attention behind his desk, forced a smile as they approached. After Adam and Kyle returned, he took his seat. "Gentlemen, I want to make it clear of my expectations."

Adam nodded while Kyle took out a few coins and played with them.

"You will take me into the future for one day so that I can see the wonders of your world. When I return, you are to destroy the chair."

"Yeah, I've been thinking about that part of the deal. I thought it read your mind and stopped you from doing that," Adam said.

"I did say that. Maybe you will have better luck in your century."

"Hey, no skin of my nose," Adam said.

"For now, our business arrangement only concerns my trip into the future."

"Yeah, that's what I said. You can crash in our place for a while. Later we'll show you around town," Adam said, still feeling unnerved by the exchange between him and Kyle.

"I expect my house staff will return any day now. So, I think we should be going." Turner rose from his chair. "We'll be needing an oil lamp for the attic."

Kyle reached into one of his trousers' cargo pockets. "You don't need it. I went into the barn yesterday and found my flashlight." He held it out and tested the light.

"That is a most unusual device," Turner said as he reached out to feel it. "It is cool to the touch, yet it resembles a torch. When I go back to my world, may I have it?"

"Sure thing," Kyle said and switched off the light.

"What about the extra batteries that you had?" asked Adam.

"Don't know. I had some in my pockets when that goon squad pulled us out of the barn."

"That's okay. We'll get some when we get home."

"Gentlemen, shall we?" Lord Turner motioned toward the door.

Kyle switched on his light and walked into the outer hall.

"Be prepared to have your socks knocked off," Adam said before following Kyle up the stairwell to the attic.

Kyle kept the beam of light from his LED flashlight squarely on the chair. In the glow, Adam and Lord Turner gathered around him.

Adam turned to Turner. "You can go first."

Turner shook his head. "I find your suggestion disconcerting and would rather have either of you two gentlemen proceed me in this great adventure."

"No problemo, your highness," Adam said. "Kyle, gimme your light. You go first, then the lord here, and I'll follow. How's that sound?"

"That is acceptable. Now let us embark on our journey through time," Turner said, who, despite his display of bravado, seemed hesitant.

After handing the flashlight to Adam, Kyle eagerly dropped back onto the chair and disappeared.

Adam waved the light's beam at the chair. "Okay, hop on and get ready for the ride of your life."

Displaying some hesitancy, Turner eased back, steadied himself on the armrests, and slowly sat down. His departure was swifter than his approach, and he, too, vanished.

With uninhibited eagerness, Adam plunked himself down and followed.

CHAPTER THIRTY-NINE

"A Good Retreat is Better Than a Bad Stand"

"What the hell?" shouted Adam as he glared at the inside of the storage locker in disbelief. The interior was as cold as the century they just left, and he assumed it was the same month.

"Where are we?" asked Lord Turner.

Kyle explored the locker with his flashlight. "How did this chair get back here?"

"Lemme have that light," demanded Adam, snatching it away from Kyle. He examined the interior side of the locking mechanism. "It's easier to break out of one of these places than break into one. The trouble is, I don't have the tools."

"What is this place?" asked Turner.

Adam continued to inspect the locking device's backplate. "It's a storage room." Eyeing Turner, he asked, "You got an adjustable wrench back at your pad?"

"By pad, I assume you mean my manor?"

"Yeah, whatever. You got one?"

"Mr. Cabano, I do not have the slightest idea of what you are referring to."

"What about a crowbar? You got one of them?"

"What does it do?" asked Turner.

"It pries things open. You know, a jimmy bar."

"Ahh, you are referring to an iron crow. I do believe we have such an implement in my stable."

"Great. Let's go back and get it," Adam said as he moved back to the chair. He looked at Turner. "I suppose you want me to go first again?"

In the LED's spillover glow, Adam saw Turner nod.

"C'mon, Kyle, let's roll."

"I ain't going."

"Wadda mean, you ain't going?"

"Hop off, man. It's the end of the line for me. I ain't moving from this place. You go, but I'm staying."

"What's the big deal? We'll only be gone for a little while."

Kyle shook his head. "It sucks back there. It was bad times, and I ain't going with you."

"Okay, okay, don't have a cow. Stay if you want, but keep your mouth shut. You understand?"

"Yeah, yeah, roger that, but I keep the flashlight."

"We need it. How we gonna see when we get to that castle?"

"Mr. Cabano, there is no need for your magic torch. I have an oil lantern in the attic. Shall we depart on our quest?" Turner said with a hint of mockery as he motioned toward the chair.

Without so much as a see you later remark, Adam jumped on the chair and disappeared into the nineteenth century.

Adam heard the shuffling of Lord Turner as Adam stumbled blindly about in the attic, trying to regain his bearings.

With a flick of a match, Turner lighted the lantern and led the way. "You are welcome to wait in my library. But I think it would be better if you accompany me—making sure I have the correct device."

"Yeah, you're right. I'll keep you company," Adam said, following in the wake of the lantern's light.

———

Kyle, alone, cold, and tired, went to a back corner of the storage locker, sat down, and turned off his flashlight. The walls of the encloser faded to black. As his eyes tried to adjust, only the slightest sliver of light crept its feeble way under the bottom edge of the door.

Shifting in place, he heard the jingle of the coins in his pocket. He reached in and pulled out a couple and began amusing himself by blindly sliding them back and forth between his thumb and forefinger. Thinking of the possible fortune he may have within his grasp and Adam's warning about keeping his mouth shut, Kyle quietly started to hum a made-up tune.

The extended wait bothered him, and the coldness of the floor made him uncomfortable. Bored, he turned on the flashlight and laid it on its side, facing himself. Kyle pulled out a fistful of coins and began to examine them. With his hand open and with ice-cold fingers, he pushed them about in the cavity of his palm, captivated by their size and impressive designs. Selecting one, he returned the rest into his pocket. Holding the lone coin, he mentally assessed its value. Flipping it into the air with self-assurance, he attempted to catch it on its downward route.

The coin bounced off the base of his thumb and rolled away into the darkness. He heard its metallic sound hit something before twirling to a stop.

Kyle rose and began to scan the interior with his flashlight. He spotted it at the base of the rolltop door. With the light fixed on the coin, he reclaimed it. Kyle returned to the corner, unconcerned by the telltale sound and the sliver of light that reached the outside.

CHAPTER FORTY

"Who Sleeps Doesn't Catch Fish"

"Do you hear that?" Morris asked Dunlap.

"Yep, and it's not making any sense. How could anyone get inside that locker without us noticing it?" asked Dunlap.

Morris moved closer to the window and looked below. "There's got to be another way in we hadn't noticed. Maybe the adjoining locker has some entryway?"

"It's a storage room," a voice said. "You got an adjustable wrench back at your pad?"

"Shh, listen?" whispered Dunlap. "Hear that? They're looking for a way to bust out. So that blows your theory."

Morris felt the hairs on the back of his head rise. "Shit. Adam Cabano and Kyle Kroft are locked in there with someone else."

"Ahh, you are referring to an iron crow. I do believe we have such an implement in my stable."

Dunlap nodded. "This is getting stranger by the minute. Who the hell is the third guy, and who talks that way? I mean, who calls something an "iron crow?"

"Yeah, you're right. Now they're going back to a manor and stable. What the hell is going on?"

"Rick, listen," Dunlap said.

"What? I don't hear anything."

"Exactly. I think they've gone somewhere."

In the faint glow from the outside street lamps, Morris glanced at his watch. "It's almost quitting time."

"You're not thinking of going, are you?" asked Dunlap.

"Of course not. I was just saying. And look who's coming."

"Yep, the night watchman," Dunlap said. "This could get interesting."

The watchman slowly moved below them, sweeping a path before him with his flashlight. Stopping at every storage building, he inspected each lock before advancing to the next. Continuing this routine until reaching the last one, the one containing the unexplained chair, he paused.

"Hear that?" asked Dunlap.

"Yeah," muttered Morris.

"The guard heard that, too," Dunlap said as she inched closer to the window.

Below them, the watchman pivoted and broke into a full run back to his shack.

Morris and Dunlap eased away from the window.

"I think this is what we came here to see," Morris said as he moved back into the shadows.

CHAPTER FORTY-ONE

"Playin' Me"

"Will this serve your needs?" asked Lord Turner, holding out the crowbar.

"It's got quite a bit of a curve to it, but it'll work," Adam said as he accepted it.

"I believe your associate may be concerned about our absence."

"Nah, he's okay. He gets a little jumpy sometimes. I think he's just tired."

"Well then, let us return. I am most eager to see your world and its wonders." Turner adjusted the flame on the lantern and proceeded toward the manor.

Adam stayed close behind as they walked along the well-worn trail back to the house. Guided by the light from the lantern, their visible breaths swirled around them in the November damp air. The path widened, and a light rain began to fall as they approached the building. Adam moved alongside Turner.

"Tell me, Mr. Cabano, what other wonders can I expect in the future?"

"Sure. We got refrigerators that keep your food cold, cars that run on gasoline, and televisions that you can see other people hundreds of miles away."

"These televisions, of which you speak, how do they work?"

"I don't really know. All you have to do is plug them into the electrical outlet, turn them on, and you see color pictures."

"That is amazing. What kind of images do you see?

"Moving pictures, like seeing you and me, only on a flatscreen."

"And these cars, are they like our wagons?" asked Turner.

"Yeah, I told you they run on gasoline."

"You mean they don't need horses to propel them?"

"Yeah, and they can go over a hundred miles an hour," Adam said, thrusting his free hand forward in a show of speed.

"I should think a day in your world may not be enough time for me to see all the marvels of your domain."

"Yeah, I know what you mean. You can crash in our place for a couple of days if you want—at no additional cost." He chuckled.

"Yes, Mr. Cabano, maybe I will."

They reached the rear entrance to the manor and quickly made their way to the attic. Among dusty discards and the time-travel chair, they were met by Lawrence and his son, Oliver. The gatekeeper carried a shotgun while his son held a lantern. Both men appeared well dressed.

"Why are they here?" asked Adam.

"They will accompany me into your world."

"I didn't agree to that. The deal was for a single round-trip ticket. And besides, don't you mean accompany us?"

"I have reconsidered our initial agreement and changed my mind."

"What about easing your conscience and smashing the chair to smithereens? And the fear the household staff will discover your, as you say, contract with a devil?"

Turner laughed. "My staff knows my business. I told you they went to help the people of Gateshead. The truth is, I didn't send them on a mission of goodwill but rather on a looting mission." He nodded to his gatekeeper and smiled wickedly. "So, you see, Mr. Cabano, you lose."

Brandishing the crowbar, Adam pulled away from Turner. Switching hands, he reached into his peacoat and pulled out his revolver. "I'm sure I've got enough slugs in this heater to drop each one of you."

Lord Turner smiled. "When you were in your drug-induced sleep, I took the liberty of removing the cylinder and extracting the pin cartridges."

Adam cocked the gun then pulled the trigger. The clink of the hammer confirmed the weapon's uselessness. Filled with rage, he repeated the process before throwing the weapon at Lord Turner.

Turner sidestepped the attack and held out his hand. "Mr. Cabano, please be so kind as to hand over the coins."

"Hey, man, you're jonking my jeter. The piggy food was part of the deal."

"I have reconsidered our agreement and decided to use them myself as barter when I go into the future. I have you to thank for the idea."

Adam pointed the chiseled-shaped end of the crowbar at Turner. "You need me to get out of that storage locker."

Turner shook his head. "Do you think we are backwoods primitives that we cannot apply the simple principle of a lever to disengage the lock?" He paused and glanced at Lawrence, his gatekeeper. "Although, I suppose your talents will be of use, and of course, to facilitate the introduction to Mr. Angelo. Oliver, get the money from the man."

The gatekeeper's son set the lantern on the floor and cautiously moved toward Adam. Lawrence raised his shotgun, level with Adam's midsection.

Adam knew he was losing options.

"Drop the iron crow and raise your hands, Mr. Cabano," demanded Turner.

Adam hurled the crowbar at Lawrence before charging toward Oliver. The gatekeeper, caught off guard, staggered and fell on his back. His gun discharged into the rough-hew timbers overhead. The recoil and unexpected action caused Lawrence to knock over the

Camphine oil lamp. The spreading oil formed a blue and red carpet of flame.

Street-smart and tough, Adam kicked Oliver in the groin. Bent over and clearly in pain, the gatekeep's son briefly provided cover. Adam then grabbed the boy, using him as a human shield during his mad dash to the chair.

Lawrence struggled to his feet. Along with Lord Turner, they both began to stomp down the growing flames. Their boots, oil-contaminated, ignited, causing them to jump about like madmen in the expanding fire. Both men, appearing crazed with fear, took off their coats and surrendered them to the blaze, seeking to smother its growth.

Leaving the boy writhing on the floor and Turner and Lawrence preoccupied, Adam snatched the crowbar. Within feet of his destination and not taking a chance of being pulled back, he dove onto the chair.

CHAPTER FORTY-TWO

"Adios Muchachos"

Adam somersaulted out of the chair and onto the storage locker's cement slab, the crowbar flying against the steel door.

Kyle's light flashed to life. "You sure took your time in getting back."

"Back off, man," Adam said while struggling to his feet. "You don't know half the shit I went through."

Kyle picked up the crowbar. "I thought you went for a bag of tools?"

"Hell, I'm lucky to have escaped with my ass intact. That lord dude turned on us. He was going to do a John Lennon act on us."

"Who's John Lennon?"

"Never mind, dipshit. Gimme that tool. We got to get outta this place before that creep comes through that chair."

"Do you think this is all you'll need?" Kyle asked, handing him the crowbar.

"Yeah, piece of cake. I just have to pry the lock and its locking arms, and we're free. C'mon, shine your light on the backplate."

With a determined thrust of the iron bar, Adam attempted to wedge its blade between the backing plate and the storage door.

"Shit!" Adam exclaimed as the sharp edge skipped off its mark.

"Aren't you worried the guard's gonna hear the noise?" asked Kyle.

"Hell, after my wipeout, everyone on Jones Island probably heard the racket. What time do you think it is?"

Kyle shrugged. "Dunno. Maybe it's late at night because it kinda quiet outside, and I don't see any light coming under the door."

"I figured that, too. If I can get this blade to set, the rest should be easy as light cheese."

"Hey, Adam."

"What?"

"Do you remember what you said about the guard?"

Adam drew back the crowbar and aimed it for another hit. "Stop moving the light. Hold it steady, shit-head. What did I say?"

"You said the watchman was takin' a booze snooze when we first broke into this place."

Adam jammed the blade of the crowbar squarely into the backplate. "There, I got it," he said and started to pull back. "Yeah, I remember. So then we don't have a thing to worry about."

"Hey," Kyle whispered, "Do you hear that?"

They both froze.

In the time between the question and the unanswered reply, the lock on the door became disengaged. The shadows of the evening unfolded before them, along with three figures backlighted in the opening.

"What the hell you guys doing in my locker?" asked Tony Angelo while Chuck, the watchman, trained his flashlight on their grimacing faces.

"Hey man, we can explain," Adam said as he backed away, one hand in submission, the other trying to conceal the crowbar behind him.

Kyle joined Adam at the rear of the locker.

From inside his heavy coat, Stephen withdrew a Smith and Wesson 9mm pistol. With his left hand, he removed an Osprey silencer from the right side of his shoulder holster's harness.

"You'll do more than explain," Tony said as he took a step forward.

Before Tony could take another step, Lawrence, the gatekeeper, materialized with his shotgun in hand. Appearing confused, he jumped free of the chair. He quickly pointed his gun at the closest target.

With reflexes quicker than a rattlesnake's, Stephen fired two hurried rounds at the gatekeeper. In response and falling backward into the chair, the gatekeeper fired his gun. Pellets ricocheted against the steel ceiling and walls. Lawrence remained less than a few seconds before disappearing.

With the swiftness of a Whac-A-Mole arcade game, Lord Turner dropped into view. Coughing and wheezing, in a cloud of smoke and looking bewildered, he surveyed the trio before him.

Appearing equally confused, Tony asked, "Who the hell are you?"

Turner brushed off traces of soot. "I, sir, am Lord Byron Turner. And to whom am I speaking to?"

"Well, I'll be damned. I'm Tony Angelo."

Turner extended his hand.

Tony ignored the gesture and closed in on Turner. "So, you decided to team up with a couple of street punks and outhustle me?"

Turner wildly searched the interior of the locker. He appeared to recognize Adam and Kyle. "Mr. Angelo, my actions were in league with your associates—Mr. Cabano and Mr. Kroft."

Tony grabbed Turner by the scruff of his neck and drew him closer. "I never saw those punks before. Don't try to bullshit me. We had a deal."

"I can explain."

"Cut the crap. I can see for myself." Tony pressed forward, tightening his grip around Turner's neck.

"Please! Let me go."

"Now, you show up with these two bums." He nodded toward Adam and Kyle. "And you bring your muscle with a shotgun."

Tony pushed Turner back against the front edge of the chair.

Looking as if he was about to lose his balance, Turner tried to counter his backward momentum by grabbing Tony's coat. The bulk of Tony and Turner's plump body acted as a counterweight against either regaining any equilibrium.

CHAPTER FORTY-THREE

"Where There's Smoke, There's Fire"

Dunlap adjusted the volume on the shotgun mic. "Can you make any sense of what they are talking about in there?"

"Hell, I'm lucky to have escaped with my ass intact. That lord dude turned on us. He was going to do a John Lennon act on us."

Morris and Dunlap eyed each other in bewilderment.

"What I want to know is how are they getting into that locker without us noticing them?" Morris asked. "And who the hell is that lord guy they're talking about?"

Dunlap nodded. "Yeah, that's a new piece of the puzzle."

Morris scratched his head. "Did you hear that? Now they're going to try to break out. Why not go back the same way you came in? Right?" He glanced at Dunlap.

Before she could meet his gaze, she exclaimed, "Look!" then pointed toward an approaching vehicle.

The car stopped briefly to pick up the nightwatchman.

"This is it," Morris said.

Under the orange glow of the sodium security lamp, Tony, Stephen, his driver, and Chuck, the night watchman, exited the black Mercedes.

The watchman removed the ring of keys from his belt and unlocked the door to the storage locker.

From above, Morris and Dunlap watched as Tony bellowed into the open void. "What the hell you guys doing in my locker?"

Unable to observe who or what was taking place inside the locker, only the angry exchange suggested it was about to come to a violent conclusion. The loud blast from a shotgun confirmed Morris's fears.

"That's it!" he shouted. "Call it in and ask for backup. I'm going down there. Cover me from up here."

"I'll follow you," Dunlap said, bringing up the two-way radio to her face.

"No! Stay put and cover me from up here."

Morris charged toward the stairwell and rushed down the steps, taking two at a time. Hitting the door's panic bar, he burst onto the sidewalk. With wild abandon, he dashed toward the alleyway behind the building.

He pushed the dumpster against the chain-link fence before scaling it. Then, after draping his leather jacket over the barbed wire, Morris jumped down to the other side. Now, jacketless, his police shield, secured on a leather badge holder, swung openly on a neck chain over his chest. He crouched down and rounded the corner, his Glock at the ready.

As Morris turned to face the storage locker's opening, illuminated by the watchman's light, he caught a glimpse of Tony Angelo as he was pulled onto a chair. Both men disappeared before his unbelieving eyes. Trapped in a moment of puzzlement, he regained his senses and yelled, "Police! Freeze!"

Stephen, still holding his Smith and Wesson 9mm pistol, turned.

Seeing the weapon, Morris let loose a salvo of rounds from his gun.

Stephen staggered backward into the chair. Then he, too, disappeared.

Chuck spun around and raised his arms. His flashlight's beam was dancing around like a light-saber in the unlit interior. He shouted, "Don't shoot! I'm not armed!"

"Okay, okay," Morris said. "Turn around and put your hands behind your back." He removed his handcuffs from their molded case, grabbed the light before snapping on the cuffs onto the watchman's wrists. Seeing Adam and Kyle, their arms raised in surrender, Morris called out to them, "C'mon out to where I can see you."

The wail of approaching sirens grew nearer.

Morris aimed the light on the two scruffy-looking men, then on the empty chair before training it on Dunlap, her Sig P226 drawn.

"Well, Detective Morris," she began, "it sounded like you did a lot of shooting, but I don't see any bodies."

"I'll explain to you later. Take care of those two." He nodded in the direction of Adam and Kyle.

Morris sniffed the air. "Something is burning." He trained the light on the chair. "Hell, the chair's starting to smoke."

"There's a fire extinguisher cabinet, a couple of lockers down," Chuck said.

"Dunlap, keep an eye on 'em," Morris ordered and ran off. Using the barrel of his Glock, he broke the glass and retrieved the extinguisher rather than use the small hammer chained to the cabinet. By the time Morris returned, flames had begun licking their way out from the center of the seat. Before the fire could spread up the back, he smothered it with a cloud of dry chemical retardant.

Several squad cars, their red and blue strobe lights flashing, began to fill the open void of Tony's storage business driveway.

CHAPTER FORTY-FOUR

"Not My Circus, Not My Monkeys"

Captain Ed Chalmers paced in front of his window as Detective Morris and Officer Dunlap looked on. Coming to a stop, he did not turn in their direction but instead looked out upon the cityscape below. "This is one for the books," Chalmers finally said. "I have two dead, according to your report, no corpses, and a partially burned chair without any bullet holes."

"That about sums it up," Morris said.

"Because of the shooting and involvement with a high-priority suspect, I'm putting you two on desk duty. The first thing I want you two to do is interview Adam Cabano and Kyle Kroft. They're in special lockup. I'm holding them for 96 hours, pending your review."

"What are you expecting us to find out from them?" asked Dunlap, who was studying her intertwined hands.

Chalmers turned. "I'm not sure. Here's the thing, Milwaukee's number one mobster, according to you two, was killed, yet we don't have a body. Do you have any idea what kind of position that puts this department in?"

Dunlap met his gaze. "I suspect a bad one."

"You're damn right it does. Without a body, autopsy, and material evidence, we are between a rock and the proverbial hard spot."

"Hey, Captain," Morris began, "I'm just as curious and eager to hear the story from those two as you are. What about the watchman? Do you want us to interrogate him, too?"

He shook his head and turned once more to look outside. "I want to be included on that one."

"Why's that?" asked Morris.

"Because he's been working at that storage facility for years. He probably knows more than anyone about the comings and goings of Tony."

"Captain, what will happen to the property? I mean, does the city take it over and sell it at auction?"

Chalmers laughed and went to his desk. After sitting down, he pulled out some papers and began to reading, commenting as he did. "The Drug Enforcement Administration can seize property if it's a federal case. The feds have been interested in Tony for years. So they will want a piece of the pie. Likewise, the State of Wisconsin. It, too, can seize property." He looked up and set the paperwork off to the side. "Tony's been suspected of running a drug operation for years. If we can get that night watchman to talk, we may get all the evidence necessary based on his testimony alone."

"How long does it take?" asked Dunlap

Chalmers glanced at the paperwork. "Ah, it looks like the state or feds have only 15 days to give notice of seizure after actually taking possession of the property. But we're getting off-topic. I want answers. Now get down there and talk to Cabano and Kroft first before we start thinking how we're going to divvy up the spoils."

———

Kyle was led into the room by a uniformed officer. After taking Kyle to the solitary chair on the far side of the room and securing his manacled hands, the cop hesitantly took up a corner position.

Morris jerked his head in the direction of the door. The policeman, obviously getting the drift, left.

Taking his seat, Morris turned on the video control that sat on the table. Dunlap followed the officer out of the room.

Alone now, Morris drummed his fingers on the table, keeping a close watch on Kyle.

Kyle fidgeted nervously in place. Like a cornered bird, he began to chirp. "Hey, man, why am I locked up? I ain't done nothin' wrong."

"Well, for one thing, you were technically trespassing."

"Ain't I suppose to have a public defender?"

"Why do you think that, considering you just told me you didn't do anything?"

"Ah, because you cops make up stuff all the time."

The door opened, and Dunlap nodded to Morris before sitting down. She took her place on the opposite side of the table. With the control console between them and a brick wall behind, they both focused their attention on Kyle.

Morris began. "I'm wondering why a small-time offender like yourself got himself mixed up with a crime boss like Tony Angelo? Were you working for Mr. Angelo?"

"Nah, nothin' like that," Kyle said, giving Dunlap a sidewise glance.

"Okay, then why were you in that locker with him?" asked Dunlap.

"Ah, you're not going to believe me."

"Try us," Morris said.

"You're gonna think I'm loco, and I'll be making baskets in the looney bin."

Morris smiled. "C'mon, give us the story."

"Okay, but when you ask Adam, he'll tell you the same thing."

Morris and Dunlap both leaned back into their chairs.

"It was Adam's idea to heist the locker."

"You mean yesterday?" Dunlap asked.

"Nah. I don't even know what day it was. Maybe we did the job two or three weeks ago."

"You don't know this, but your sister contacted us because she was worried about you," Dunlap said.

"Kate?" asked Kyle, appearing stunned.

"Yes," Dunlap began. "Your sister, Katharine, contacted the Milwaukee Police Department and reported you as missing. She loves you and was very worried—"

"Which brings us to ask," Morris interrupted, "where were you and Adam hiding out?"

"Okay, this is the shit that you're gonna think I was robotripping."

"We're listening," Morris said.

"I'll be straight. We were time-hopping in Victorian England. That's where the barmaid said we were."

There were a few seconds of silence. Morris and Dunlap traded glances.

"Yeah, I knew you wouldn't believe me."

"We didn't say anything. It's just a bit ... incredible," Morris said.

Kyle's demeanor brightened. "Hey, I got proof."

"Like what?" asked Dunlap.

"When I got checked into your Hilton, the cop made me empty my pockets. He took all my piggy money."

"Piggy money?" Morris asked.

"Yeah, coins ... my English coins."

"What does that prove?"

"That was part of the deal with that dude, lord. That was my share of the Willy Wonka's golden ticket to our time. Adam got the other half. See, we said he could come and stay in our pad for a day or two. That was the price of admission, the piggy money, I mean."

"How did you get to Victorian England in the first place, and what did you do there?" asked Morris.

"Yeah, that's the goofy part. We traveled in that chair we heisted from the locker. I made the first trip and came back. It was like traveling on a fast train or rollercoaster. When I told Adam about the spooky *Addam's Family* house, he wanted to go, too. Then he figured we'd score some stuff and bring back the loot and fence it here in Milwaukee. Things got awkqueerd."

"What do you mean?" Dunlap asked.

"Well, first off, Adam says he didn't really kill those guys in the past because they were already dead."

Morris, who had been slowly inching his way closer, suddenly jerked back into the chair and began scratching his head with both hands. "Who did he kill?" he asked with an insistent tone.

"The first guy was a night watchman, and the second dude was a bartender."

Morris looked at Dunlap, rolled his eyes, and shook his head. Without saying another word, he reached over and turned off the recorder.

"Okay, I heard enough," Morris began. "Right now, we have you and Adam on charges of trespassing. Since Tony Angelo is missing and unable to press charges, you'll probably walk."

There was a knock.

Dunlap rose and opened the door. "Miss Kroft, please have a seat." She gestured toward the only other available chair set off to the side.

Kyle's complexion turned crimson.

"Earlier, I called your sister to let her know we found you," Morris said.

Kyle fidgeted in place while Morris and Dunlap quietly consulted.

Dunlap nodded to Morris.

Morris turned on the recorder. "Okay, this is what we are offering you," he began. "Kyle Kroft, we are releasing you into the custody of your sister. You, most likely, will be called upon to testify in the future. Other than keeping your nose clean, we have one condition."

"What's that?"

Dunlap glanced at Katharine Kroft and gave her a nod before turning back to Kyle. "You're also prohibited from making contact with Adam Cabano."

Katharine Kroft smiled.

"What about all my coins?" Kyle asked.

"The guard will return everything after you are processed. You have to sign some paperwork first. Now your sister will go and wait for you on the main floor."

Kyle's sister rose and moved toward the exit. She gave her brother a warm smile before being escorted out.

"Mr. Kroft, you didn't give us an answer. Will you abide by the conditions?" Morris asked.

"Yeah, sure," Kyle answered meekly.

"I'll get the guard," Dunlap said.

After handing him off, Dunlap returned to her seat. "You know better than I on this one. Considering what you told me and Tony's disappearance, along with Kyle's statement, how are you going to explain all this?"

Morris shook his head. "I can't. From what I have already heard, the forensics team is having a hard time matching some of the shooting evidence. No surprise there. The problem—two types of shell casings and the absence of shotgun shells. Of course, they have only identified my Glock."

She nodded. "Yeah, a gun fired in a compartment with no concrete evidence except your spent round casings and lead shotgun pellets is a hard one to document. I'm sure the boys and girls in the lab are spending a lot of time scratching their heads on this one."

"Yeah, we got to get going. The captain wants to be in on the interview with the watchman. We'll talk with Adam Cabano and see how his story meshes with Kyle's. But before that, let's have a look at Kyle's 'piggy money' and see what other treasures they had in their pockets."

CHAPTER FORTY-FIVE

"Two Wrongs Don't Make a Right"

The red light on the recording system shone brightly in the unadorned interior of the interrogation room. Again, Morris and Dunlap sat across from one another, a narrow table dividing them with one end secured to the wall.

Morris picked up a clipboard. "Tell us, why were you in that storage locker with Tony Angelo?"

Adam, his attitude defiant, sat at the far end of the room and leaned back in his chair, his movement curtailed by the short length of his chained restraint. "Listen, man, I'll tell you again, we traveled back in time. There was this Lord Turner, who was going to come back with us—you know, to the present."

"When I came around the corner, I only saw Tony's driver, Stephen. Where was Tony, and this make-believe Lord Turner?" Morris said.

"Hey, man, he was real. Before you showed up, Tony and that lord guy got into it. You know, real physical. Tony accuses that Turner guy of trying to outhustle him. Before you know it, they're both taking a dive back to England—through the chair."

"Your pal, Kyle, told me you killed a couple of guys. Is that true?" asked Morris.

Adam shouted defiantly, "You can't charge me with a murder committed in 1854."

"So, you did kill someone?" Dunlap asked forcefully.

"I ain't talking. I want a public defender."

Morris deferred the subject with a dismissive wave. "Okay, we don't have to talk about that now. What was so special about the chair? I mean, how was it able to send you back in time?"

"That lord guy, he said he bought it from someplace in France. I forgot the name of the town. He said it was cursed and had the power to send things through time."

Morris jotted down a note then looked up at Adam. "That doesn't sound like that's a curse."

"Yeah, that's what I said. But he tells me he traded some art and other stuff for electronic things for his pal, Joseph Swan."

"Joseph Swan?" Dunlap cried.

"Yeah, the guy said he was some kind of inventor."

Morris shot Dunlap a look of surprise. "You heard of him?"

Dunlap nodded. "Yeah, he was a famous English inventor. In England, he's considered the inventor of the electric light bulb—years ahead of Edison."

Morris laughed. "You continue to amaze me with your knowledge. And we seem to be off message. Besides the electrical stuff, Adam, what other things did he trade in?"

Adam cleared his throat. "Bodies."

Morris jerked back. "Bodies? You do mean dead bodies, don't you?"

"Yeah," Adam retorted. "You cops are supposed to be smart. There's only one kind of body that I know, and it's a dead body."

Once more, the exchange stopped cold while Morris tried to process the admission. Following a long silence, he asked, "Did you see any of those bodies?"

"Nah, he told me he'd put them six feet under in his back yard, or whatever he called his Bonanza spread."

"So, what you are telling us is that Lord Turner was a racketeer?" asked Morris.

"That's affirmative. And when that town, ah ... Gateshead, explodified, he sent his peeps to loot the place."

Morris exhaled and glanced at Dunlap. He turned off the audio and video machine.

"Listen," Morris began, "I told your pal, Kyle, the only thing I could charge him with is trespassing. That requires the owner to file a complaint."

"Hey, Tony Angelo took a trip in that chair. So, I'm free. Right?"

"Listen, punk," Morris snapped. "Not so fast. I wouldn't be so confident if I were you. You were carrying a concealed weapon."

"What weapon?"

Morris reached into his pocket and pulled out an ornate letter opener, sealed in a plastic evidence bag. He waved it at Adam. "This," he said tauntingly.

"Hell, that ain't no weapon."

"It's a matter of perspective," chimed Dunlap.

"Let's say, for argument sake, we forget about this," Morris began, laying down the bag on the table. "I think you got more things to worry about, other than a concealed weapons offense."

"Like what?"

"You see, smart ass, you're the last guy to see Tony alive."

"What does that have ... ."

Morris smiled and nodded. "Yeah, now you get it. What do you think is going to happen to you once the word is out on the street?"

"Hey, man. You're the only ones who know that. You wouldn't spread that kind of shit about me, would you?"

"Don't be so sure about that. I gave Kyle a choice, and I'm going to give you one, too."

Adam's eyes grew wild. "What kind of choice?"

"Once we release you, I'd suggest you get out of Dodge while you still can. Tony's friends are going to be looking for answers. And right now, I'm glad I'm not in your shoes."

Adam's faced turned ashen. "I need money to blow this town."

"Before our little meeting, here," Dunlap began, "I looked over those coins that Kyle said you got from your pal Lord Turner."

"Yeah, so what? I didn't steal them. He gave them to me. It was the price of the fare to the future," Adam said, his words rattled off in a succession of nervous bursts.

"I know the value of things," Dunlap said. "Including the gold and silver coins, you probably have a small fortune. That should give you enough dough to start a new life somewhere else."

Morris chimed in. "Oh, I forgot to mention this. You are not to see Kyle ever again."

"Hey, man, he's my wingman. We're a team."

"Not anymore, if you get my drift," Morris shot back. "You know what I said about Tony's friends?"

"Yeah."

"If you so much as get within two blocks of Kyle, I'll spread the word on the street that you wacked Tony and his driver."

"You wouldn't do that."

"You wanna bet?" Morris thundered. "Now, after you leave, I'd suggest you find yourself a coin dealer. With the money you get, buy yourself a one-way ticket to someplace where you can blend in—like, maybe a swamp in Florida."

Morris called for the guard to take Adam away.

"That's two down and one more to go," Morris said as he shuffled his notes together.

"Are we going to use this interrogation room again when we interview the night watchman?" asked Dunlap.

"No. Captain Chalmers wants it held in his office."

"Isn't that unusual, considering the watchman may be criminally involved? Besides, he doesn't have the recording capabilities in his office."

"Yeah, I thought so, too, and raised the same question. But that's the way he wants it. C'mon, let's go upstairs and see what he's up to."

———

When Morris and Dunlap entered Captain Chalmers' office, they found him sitting erect behind his desk. On the left side of the room and only a few feet away from the captain's desk sat two stoic-looking men. They each favored shades of black in their suit attire, punctuated with ebony ties against their snowy white shirts.

Chalmers remained seated. With a wave of his hand, he motioned toward the men. "This is Special Agent Willow and Special Agent Birch. They're from the FBI's International Organized Crime Intelligence's Division." Redirecting his hand, he motioned. "And this is Detective Morris and Officer Dunlap. They've been working on the Angelo case."

Neither man rose or extended a hand, delivering only an acknowledging nod.

"Willow and Birch, an interesting combination," quipped Morris.

"You're the first person to mention that," Agent Willow countered sarcastically.

Chalmers fired Morris a look of disapproval. "Why don't you two have a seat."

"I thought we were going to be in on the interrogation of the watchman?" Morris asked as he began to sit.

The captain shot forward with such swiftness that Morris felt the only thing that saved him was the desk between them. "There's no need for that," he said tersely.

"Why?" Morris fired back.

"Listen, this is no longer a Milwaukee Police Department matter," Chalmers said, turning a shade of red. "The night watchman told us everything. He is now in the process of being relocated under the U.S. Federal Witness Protection Program."

"Hey, Captain, with all due respect to both you and Agents Willow and Birch," Morris said, displaying a mocking smile. "Isn't that administered by the U.S. Marshals Service?"

"Yeah, and the FBI's been trying to put Tony Angelo away for years. So, they have an interest in Tony. They're here to put a bow on it."

"I'm getting the drift the case is closed?" Morris asked.

"Yep, you're right," Chalmers agreed. "We learned that Tony, among his other underworld dealings, was in the business of making bodies disappear for the Mob. That was his moneymaker. The watchman told us he helped Tony and his driver place bodies into that end storage locker. It served as a temporary holding site until being moved to a final resting spot."

"What about the chair?" asked Morris.

Chalmers snapped back. "What does that have to do with anything?"

Morris glanced at Dunlap, who appeared just as mystified. "Um ... I just thought you wanted to know what we found out from Cabano and Kroft."

"Like what?" Chalmers asked.

A dark thought came over Morris. He wanted to use his loaner gun to erase the FBI agents' haughty attitude, who appeared to display amusement at the exchange. "Ah, it was nothing. It was about the antique business Tony was running. I'll tell you later, Captain."

"Yeah, small stuff by comparison to Tony's undertaker business."

The FBI agents rose.

"Captain Chalmers, it's been a pleasure," Agent Willow said while extending a parting hand. Agent Birch followed suit. Neither of the men glanced at Morris or Dunlap, leaving in a small procession taking with them their smugness.

No sooner did the door close than Chalmers, in a gruff voice, ordered, "Dunlap, why don't you go and get yourself a cup of coffee. And take your time."

She promptly rose, meeting Morris's eyes with a quizzical expression before leaving.

Chalmers leaned back in his chair and folded his arms over his chest. "Well, I don't mind when you step on your dick, but when you step on my dick, I'm gonna yell."

"What do you mean, Captain?"

"You're a good cop, but that only gets you so much freedom. When you did your smartass routine in front of those agents, it undermines my authority."

"But—"

"But, nothing. A little advice, ... no, a lot of advice, rather than running off that mouth of yours, wait to see if someone has something to say first. Do you understand?"

Morris knew he had it coming and didn't reply, hoping the silence would suffice for his remorse.

Chalmers pressed for a reply. "Do you understand?"

"Yeah," he answered, letting his wounded gaze drop to the floor.

"Don't you think I read your incident report? How do you think those FBI guys would react to the disclosure about Tony disappearing into a chair?"

"Um—"

"I'll tell you how they would react. They would leave here with bigger smiles than they did. This police force, you and I included, would become the laughingstock for years."

"Captain, I saw what I saw."

Chalmers sighed, and his arms dropped to his side. "Yeah, I know you did. I saw the surveillance tape. I never shared those tapes with the Feds."

"Okay, now what?"

"Both you and Dunlap are on administrative leave until after the inquest. But I want you and Dunlap to meet me somewhere."

"Whereto?" Morris asked.

"That storage locker. I want to check out that chair for myself."

CHAPTER FORTY-SIX

"Playing with Fire"

Lord Turner, forced backward under the weight of Tony Angelo, fell onto the gatekeeper. The gatekeeper, writhing in pain, moaned.

Tony, his arms still on Turner's coat, pushed himself free. Before he could step away, Oliver, the gatekeeper's son, called out to him.

Tony turned.

Having retrieved his father's shotgun, he broke open the gun's breach to reload.

"You shot my father!" the boy screamed as he stood only a few feet away from Tony.

"Listen, kid. Put that down!"

Tony reached inside his coat. As his hand cleared the edge of his lapel, the pistol became visible.

Oliver pulled the trigger.

With arms outstretched, Tony staggered backward, his gun flying from his hand. Tony's midsection, bombarded with buckshot, dripped crimson.

Once more, Turner felt the weight of Tony as it collapsed upon him.

He shoved the body away—his clothing now spotted with blood. Turner cried out, "Oliver, help me."

As the boy approached, the body of Stephen tumbled free of the chair and onto the attic floor.

With reflex swiftness, Oliver reloaded and aimed his shotgun at the fallen man.

Stephen did not move.

Oliver stepped cautiously around the bodies. He picked up Tony's discarded gun and shoved it into his waistband before setting his own shotgun aside. He helped Turner to his feet.

"Come on, lad, we have to put out this fire," Lord Turner commanded.

"Sir, after you left, we had it under control."

"Enough talk, for now. Quick, help me remove these coats," Turner said, trying to pull the heavy winter coats from the fallen men.

As they yanked the garments free, a tongue of flame reached the chair and quickly spread to its seat.

"The chair! The chair!" Turner called out.

Clutching Tony's thick overcoat, Turner thrust it onto the flames. With a great deal of effort, he successfully suppressed the fire. As the chair smoldered, he noted the coat did not disappear.

He drew back and removed the coat. Smoke swirled to the rafters. Turner's eyes followed the cloud to the trusses and became conscious that a downpour began to pelt the roof above.

Turner noticed Oliver weeping over his wounded father. "Step lively, lad, help me open the windows," he shouted.

Oliver showed a sign of hesitation.

"Now, boy. We'll tend to your father later. If we don't extinguish this fire, we shall all perish."

With Turner in the lead, they rushed to the end gable. Having opened the thumb latch that held the frames together, Turner tried to push open the window sash. Years of unuse now made the task impossible. The rainfall ran in torrents against the glass.

"Come on, boy, give me a hand."

Attempting to use their full force against the stubborn sash, it failed to yield. One of the windowpanes broke under pressure, and a draft began to flow through the attic.

Turner glanced back to see the floorboards flame up. "Hurry before we all die," Turner yelled and rushed back to retrieve the chair.

Turner and Oliver pushed it, seat forward, in front of the window.

"Come, boy, lift it," Turner commanded.

They each grabbed a side. Like a battering ram, they began to strike at the frame.

"Harder, boy, harder," Turner urged.

More glass panes broke as they struck the window several times before the center of the frame gave way. The updraft from the open trapdoor rushed past them. The smoldering fabric hissed as the rain began to cover the chair. For a brief moment, it teetered on the windowsill before being flung to the ground.

Turner grabbed Tony's coat again. He placed it in the path of the rain. Even with the strong draft rushing past them from below, the rain continued to pour through the gable. "Oliver, we need water on the floor."

In a pleading voice, rising over the clamor of falling rain, Lawrence called out. "Help me!"

"Sir, my father's badly injured."

"Yes, yes, of course. Go now. Fetch your mother and tell her to bring a bucket."

There was some hesitation as Oliver looked back at his father.

"Go, lad. Hurry," Turner shouted and began to cough as the smoke swirled about him.

Oliver, skirting the growing flames, rushed downstairs.

Now alone, Turner, his breathing labored and gasping for air, began to use the coats, even his own, to capture the rain. Alternating soaking them, then throwing them onto the flames.

Lawrence's groaning became more insistent as the flames widened toward him.

CHAPTER FORTY-SEVEN

"Skeptics Are Never Deceived"

A cutting current of damp Lake Michigan air shrouded Jones Island as Captain Chalmers exited his command car. A thin layer of snow covered the ground. Unchallenged by the two uniformed officers who sat in their squad car, he made his way to the watchman's shack. Once inside, Detective Morris was the first to greet him.

"Good afternoon, Captain," Morris said, rising from his swivel chair and setting aside his Styrofoam cup of coffee.

Dunlap, already standing at attention, echoed Morris's welcome.

"Well, I'm here. Show me this wonder chair that can make people disappear."

"Sure thing, Captain," Morris said before slipping on a pair of black leather gloves. He grabbed a flashlight off the desk and led the way outside.

The new snow cover, blemished by tracks of previous callers, crunched under their feet as they moved to the rear of the lot.

"I'll tell you what," Chalmers began, "the only reason I came out here on this crappy day was to satisfy my curiosity. Also, I would have picked a better day if it wasn't for the news—the Feds are taking over the property."

"When?" Dunlap asked.

"On Monday."

Using the unlit flashlight, Morris pointed to the last locker. "The chair is in there, Captain. So, I take it all these tracks are from the U.S. Treasury people?"

"Yeah," answered Chalmers. "Considering its location, there's going to be a lot of interest in this property. It's what the real estate people call choice."

"What about Tony Angelo's wife? Doesn't she get some of the money off the sale?" asked Dunlap.

The captain shook his head. "Normally, the wife has some protection and rights to the proceeds. But, in Tony's case, and the fact that it's Tony's third wife, he didn't include her in the title."

"Burned twice, learned thrice," mocked Morris, then laughed.

Both Chalmers and Dunlap shot him a glance.

"Hey, it's just a joke," he countered.

"Go ahead, Morris, break the seal," ordered the captain.

Following the breaking of the seal, he squirreled it into his jacket pocket.

The rollers squealed in their tracks as Morris lifted the door. "There it is, Captain."

Chalmers sniffed the cold air. "It smells kinda funny."

Morris turned on his flashlight and aimed its beam at the partially charred chair. "Yeah, it's probably the horsehair they used to stuff them years ago."

The captain followed the shaft of light and cautiously touched an arm of the chair.

"I'd be careful, Captain," warned Morris. "The last guy who touched it disappeared."

"So, you say." Chalmers turned toward him, and Morris promptly let the beam drop to the floor. "Here's the thing. I had to change your report."

"Like, how?"

"Like, the part where you come around the corner and see Tony do a disappearing act."

"So, what did you report?"

"The report states that when you arrived, you witnessed him being forced into a van by a rival gang. Someone in the truck drew their weapon, but you fired first, possibly wounding one of the men before they sped away. That would account for the spent casing and no bullets."

"What about Stephen, his driver? How did you explain his disappearance?"

Chalmers turned away. The whole matter made him uncomfortable, and he was short on answers. "He was already taken out by the rival gang when you got there, and—."

"Hey, Captain," Dunlap interrupted. "What about the audio and videotapes? They don't support your account."

He turned to meet her gaze. "Here's the thing. Do you really think your explanation is believable? Sure, your story sorta rings true, but when it comes down to explaining the disappearance of Tony Angelo and his driver, it ain't gonna sell on the street. When we get back to the station, all you have to do is sign the revised report."

Dunlap protested, "But, the recordings?"

Chalmers turned toward the chair. "The soundtracks with the corresponding footage turned out to be corrupted. As a result, they were unusable."

"All of them?" Morris asked.

Chalmers didn't reply. He reached out and touched the chair. "What's supposed to happen?"

"Adam Cabano and Kyle Kroft said the chair felt electrical," Morris said.

"Well, I don't feel anything." Chalmers reached into his pocket and pulled out a fistful of coins. Selecting a quarter, he flipped it onto the seat, where it remained.

Morris redirected his flashlight on the coin.

After a few seconds of staring, Chalmers picked up the quarter. Without hesitating, he spun around and sat on the partially burned seat. Even in the subdued light of the flashlight's indirect beam, he could see Morris and Dunlap's shocked expressions. He spread his arms in triumph. "See, nothing."

CHAPTER FORTY-EIGHT

"Time to Read"

"What's so important in the library that you want me to come here on my off day?" asked Morris.

"You'll see," Dunlap said, stepping off the escalator. She examined him with some curiosity. "Don't tell me. This is your first time in the library."

"No, it isn't," he retorted. "I came here on a class trip when I was in high school."

Dunlap's laugh caused a few of the library's patrons to look in their direction. "How is it that you, a detective, never come here to research at least once and a while?"

"Everything I need I get off the department's internet server."

"Well, like your new-found pastime of jogging, which I may add, I introduced you to, welcome to the world of historical research."

"So, we came here to look through some old books?"

"A few," she answered. "I scheduled an appointment to view some of the Milwaukee Public Library's archives."

"You hafta make an appointment to look at some old books? I thought all you had to do is come here and pick a book off the shelf."

"No," she whispered, "you have to schedule an appointment 24 hours in advance.

Christmas trimmings decorated the Visitor Service's desk.

A matronly woman looked up as they approached. Although the area was warm, she wore a buttonless red cardigan sweater interwoven with reindeer figures. Her badge indicated her name as Veronica. She looked up. "Oh," she said, eyeing Dunlap with surprise. "Back again, ah ... Susan, isn't it?"

"Yes, it is, and this is my friend Rick Morris. We're here to look through your rare books collection again."

The clerk nodded at Morris, punched a few keys, then looked up. "Yes, I see your reservation. First, I need to see both of your identifications."

While Veronica began to type, Dunlap pulled out her driver's license and laid it on the counter. Morris started to take out his police ID. Dunlap shook her head, pointed to his driver's license, and then nodded.

With the formalities out of the way, they proceeded to the rare books section.

"Why did you stop me from using my police creds?" Morris asked.

"Because not everyone likes police officers. Unfortunately, that's a fact of life nowadays. And, besides, using the public library doesn't require a search warrant. It would be a bit of an overkill."

Sealed off from the rest of the library by a glass wall, they made their way into the Krug Rare Books Room.

"What are you looking for?" asked Morris.

Dunlap smiled. "I'm not looking for anything. I already found it."

"Okay, I'll play your game of twenty questions. What have you found?"

"I found the answer and end of our investigation." She moved past the ornate shelving ends and turned into one of the aisles. "It's right over here."

Dunlap reached for an archival container from the shelf. "Here it is," she said, waving it in the air. "Let's have a seat, and I'll show what I've found." She led him to a set of comfortable-looking chairs.

"Well, this is cozy. Not what I expected to see in a library," Morris said before sitting down.

Dunlap joined him in the adjacent seat. "Now, I started to do some research about the Victorian era around the time of Adam and Kyle's visit. They talked about the fire at Newcastle and Gateshead. So, I limited my search to that time and place. I found a book on the internet covering that timeframe and location. I discovered that the library had an original copy. We could have viewed it online, but I thought this would be more fun."

Morris nodded. "I'm impressed."

"Besides, old books sometimes have notes written in their margins that make each copy unique." She removed the book from its protective case and placed it on her lap. "This book, *A Record of the Great Fire in Newcastle and Gateshead*, not only talks about that fire, but it sheds light on the region and its people—including outbreaks of cholera."

"Okay, but what does cholera hafta do with our investigation?"

Dunlap smiled. "Nothing. Besides the fire and outbreaks of diseases, what is interesting are the footnotes and charts."

"What's so interesting about stats?"

"Rick, the devil's in the details. First of all, it documents the specifics of life during the time, and second, the footnotes add an interesting comment to the subject material. And that leads me to this." She opened the book and flipped through several pages. "Take a look at this." She handed him the volume. "Right there, in the middle. Go ahead and read it out loud."

Morris cleared his throat. "Near Boldon New Winning, in 1854, near the time of the Great Fire of Newcastle and Gateshead, a fire broke out at the estate of Lord Byron Turner, merchant, killing him, his gatekeeper, and two unidentified individuals." He paused.

"Rick, go ahead and read the footnote."

"The estate of Lord Turner was destroyed. The identity of the unnamed men remains a mystery, and the items on their person were found to be peculiarly interesting. The charred remains offered no further clues except for the unique quality of their shoes." He looked up. "Wow, now that's interesting, but I have one problem with this."

"What's that?"

He closed the book and looked at its cover. "The published date is 1855. How's it possible that Tony and his driver get sucked up into the nineteenth century and get mentioned in this book?"

"That's a good question, for which I don't have an answer."

"Okay, I'll ask it another way," began Morris. "If you had come here before we got involved in this case, would the wording be the same? I mean, the part about the unidentified men—would it be there?"

She nodded. "Now that's also a good question, Rick. You know what?"

"What?"

"That's probably going to dog me the rest of my life."

"Yeah, me, too," he said, handing her the book.

CHAPTER FORTY-NINE

"All of Life's Trials are Unexpected"

Susan Dunlap fingered the zipper pull on her down jacket. "Rick?"

Morris returned his Styrofoam coffee cup to its holder. "Yeah?"

A couple of vehicles shot past Morris's parked Subaru, spattering its side with salt-laden slush.

"I've been meaning to ask you something," she said with hesitation.

He looked at her. "Yeah? Go ahead and ask."

"Now, don't get the wrong idea."

"Don't tell me. You asked Captain Chalmers for a transfer to some other detective."

She shook her head. "No, that's not it. Ah ... I don't have any friends here in Milwaukee."

He laughed. "Yeah, neither do I."

She greeted his sarcasm with a smile. "You know what I mean. Be serious for once."

"Okay, go ahead."

She continued to play with her zipper. "In the short time we've been partners, you never said anything about having a girlfriend."

"Yeah, who's got the time with the goofy schedule? It didn't go that well when I was married. So, I guess I'm sorta married to my job for now. Why you ask?"

"Well, that's good—I mean about the part you're not seeing anyone. Before I mess this up, I was wondering if you would like to have Christmas dinner with me?"

He looked at her and smiled. "That depends. Are you going to have turkey or ham, or is it going to be a vegan meal?"

"You know, Rick, I can understand your single status."

"You're referring to my charm, aren't you?"

Susan burst out laughing. "Yeah, your charm. So, Mister Wiseguy, whaddaya say? I'll be serving turkey *and* ham."

"I say yes, and I'll bring the wine." He picked up his cup and waved it in her direction.

"You know, Rick, this stakeout on the stash house isn't as exciting as the last case we were on."

"Tell me," he agreed. "I don't think we'll ever get another case as exciting as that one. And it was the most bizarre case, too."

"Whatever happened to Tony's storage facility? I mean, was it sold?"

"Yeah. I asked Captain Chalmers the same thing yesterday. The Department of Justice can move pretty fast when it wants to."

"And the chair?"

"I guess it went to the new owner. You know, I was half expecting Chalmers to be zipped away when he sat down on it."

"Yeah, that was pretty brave of him."

"Or stupid," Rick quipped.

"I thought it was brave of him."

"I don't think he really believed everything that happened. When you think about it, would you believe it if someone told you that story?"

"Probably not. I'm sure that's why he amended the report."

"I saw Tony disappear and still find it hard to believe."

Dunlap nodded. "Yeah. Did you ever consider it may have something to do with the kind of person who sat on the chair?"

"What do you mean?" he asked.

"I mean, Captain Chalmers is an upright kind of guy. Kyle, Adam, Tony, and his driver—not so much."

"So you're saying it has something to do with the character of the cargo or the operative?"

"Could be. Who knows?"

Morris smiled. "Well, I'm not going back there to test your theory. Not sure I want to take the chance."

Dunlap laughed and picked up the binoculars from the center console. She trained them on the drug house. "What time does our relief get here?"

"Eleven."

She set the binoculars aside. "Ah ... there's something else I want to tell you."

"Nothing serious, I hope."

"Remember when we went to the art museum?"

"Yeah?"

"Well, you remember Paul Bender, the Director of European Art?"

"Yeah, that pompous ass?

"Not exactly my assessment of him, but yeah. Anyway, he contacted me and told me there was an opening for the museum's Public Relations Manager slot."

He studied her and felt uneasy. "I think I know what you're going to tell me."

She nodded. "Yes, it was too good of an opportunity to pass up."

"So, now what?"

"Rick, I'm going to submit my resignation tomorrow with a two-week notice."

Morris turned away, gazing listlessly at the snow-covered street. He held his thoughts for a moment. Without turning back, he said, "I know I'm not the best person to work with, but you have been my best partner. Take that for what it's worth."

She cleared her throat. "Thanks, Rick."

"Our Christmas dinner is still on, isn't it?"

Susan laughed. "Sometimes, Rick, you're a real idiot."

"I take that as a compliment."

"As were my intentions. Yeah, our Christmas dinner is still on, and who knows where that will lead."

He looked at her. "Dessert?"

She smiled.

CHAPTER FIFTY

"A Bad Beginning Makes for a Bad Ending"

Once covered with a blanket of pristine snow, Milwaukee's streets now looked dirty, compressed under a layer of ice, road salt, and exhaust soot. The early January thaw that brought out the winter-weary citizens only a few days ago now found the self-isolation of the indoors more to their liking after the sudden drop in temperature.

With the holidays over, curbsides became littered with discarded tinsel-laden Christmas trees and other seasonal castoffs. Only those required to leave the shelter of their homes ventured outside. Vehicles moved slowly as their tires crunched through frozen rutted pathways.

Dewey picked his nose while steering his Ford stake and platform truck with the other hand. "Ya see, Shorty, all this stuff people shit-can is good stuff. People are stupid. Now, look at that stove." Slowing his vehicle, he pointed with his previously nose-occupied hand. "It's perfectly good. Sure, the color's olive green, but I'll lay you ten-to-one —it can make a pot of coffee or bake a pie. C'mon, let's grab it."

Dewey slipped on a pair of stained leather gloves. While the Ford idled, its exhaust creating a thick fog in the frigid air, he joined Shorty, who was busy examining the stove. "Looks good, doesn't it?" Dewey asked, gesturing toward the appliance.

Shorty nodded. "Let's get this on the truck before I freeze my ass off."

Dewey opened the tailgate. "Yeah, sure, I forgot you're a wimp." He tipped the stove slightly on its side while Shorty grabbed the bottom edge.

"I ain't no wimp. I can't see standing in the friggin cold admiring an old stove."

They slid the stove forward onto the nearly loaded flatbed before going back to the warmth of the truck's cab.

Dewey discarded his gloves on the dashboard. He wiped his runny nose with his jean jacket's sleeve. "Shorty, you got the muscle, and I got the vision."

"Yeah, sure, but that doesn't mean shit when I'm freezing. I don't know why we're out here when it's so dang cold?"

"Because this is the time we score big on people's throw-outs—right after the holidays. Most of the other pickers come out only in the warmer weather."

Shorty cupped his hands and blew into them.

Once more, Dewey brought his hand to his face. This time, using his thumb, he picked at his nose.

Shorty turned away and gazed out the window. "When are we going back to the shop?"

"We got room for one more. I want to make this—" Dewey halted mid-sentence. "Well, well, there's our last prize of the night." The vehicle slowed, then stopped next to a chair.

"Dewey, maybe you can't see it from your side, but the chair has a big burn mark on it."

"Hell, like a new coat of paint on a worn cabinet, it only needs a change of fabric."

———

After parking the Ford, Dewey closed the massive garage doors. There was an eclectic collection of appliances, furniture, and a mix of the flotsam and jetsam scavenged from the streets of Milwaukee in the next bay. He appreciatively eyed the contents of the truck. "Hell, we made a pretty good haul this time."

"We gonna offload now?"

Dewey shook his head. "Nah ... it's getting late. We can do it tomorrow."

"Sounds all right by me," Shorty said, his breath visible in the unheated garage.

"Yeah, go-ahead. I'll lock up."

"Thanks. I'm heading home to a nice hot shower and some schnapps."

"Hell, why wait till you get home? I got some schnapps here. Consider it a job well-done drink." Dewey patted Shorty on the back and moved past the truck and toward the office.

Dewey's domain, crammed with a government-style gray metal desk, a couple of mismatched filing cabinets, walls with clipboards commingled with nude pinups, was tight but cozy warm. He reached down and opened a door on the side of the desk, and pulled out a bottle of peppermint schnapps. He filled a coffee-stained porcelain cup a quarter of the way.

Shorty removed a glass from a shelf, blew into it, then held it out, smiling. "Hit me," he said.

After a celebratory clink, both men downed the contents.

Following some lip-smacking, Dewey asked, "One more for the road?"

Before Shorty could answer, there was a rattle of metal coming from the garage. "What the hell was that?" Dewey asked.

Shorty shrugged. "Don't know. This time of year, maybe it's a rat." He placed his glass on the desk. He followed Dewey, who had pushed past him on his way to the garage.

Dewey, in the lead, flipped on the light switch. A figure moved in the shadows between the truck's tailgate and the garage door. Dewey snatched a tire iron off the workbench. "Come out where I can see you," he ordered.

A young man moved from behind the truck. His clothing was loose-fitting and peculiar. In his hand, he held a revolver.

Both Dewey and Shorty checked their advance.

"How'd you get in here?" asked Dewey before retreating slightly. He tightened his grip on the tire iron. "Hey, kid, what the hell do you want?"

"You're the men who killed my father!" yelled the boy before firing the gun.

Postscript

"There are some journeys you do not realize you are on until they are nearly over."
Baron Friedrich von Berger

ACKNOWLEDGMENTS

Eileen Malinger,
The Lady Lake Chapter and Oxford Chapter
of the Florida Writers Association, and
Sean Malinger

ABOUT THE AUTHOR

Christopher Malinger lives with his wife Eileen, in Central Florida. His works include, *The Object of Desire*, which appeared in *Journeys VII*; an Anthology of Award-Winning Short Stories, published in 2014. Also, he was a winner of the Florida Writers Association's Adult Collection, Volume 7, *The Sweet Scent of Spring; published in 2015*. And again in 2017, his short story, *Iggy*, was included in the 2017 Florida Writers Association's Adult Collection. In 2018 he was voted one of the top ten writers in the Florida Writers Association's Adult Collection, Volume 10, for his short story, *A Story Teller's Tale*. In 2019, the theme of the collection was, *Writers at Work* for which he won placement again for his story, *Inspiration*. At the time of this current printing of 2020, he was included in Volume 12, for his story *Jealousy*.

Other works include *Cat's Paw*, a fictional account of the bombing of British European Airline's Flight 284, published in 2016. A collection of short stories, *Tales to Keep You Awake, The Back Roads of Terror,* and his novella, *The Wabele,* which won second place for general fiction in the 2017 annual Florida Writers Association Royal Palm Literary award's contest. In 2019, *Scrubbed* received the Silver Award for the unpublished (at the time) novella category.

He is a member of the Florida Writers Association.

www.ingramcontent.com/pod-product-compliance
Lightning Source LLC
Chambersburg PA
CBHW050528260626
47157CB00004B/1509